GENESIS SEQUENCE

AN ACROSS HORIZONS ORIGIN

STAN C. SMITH

A Skyra Publication

Copyright © 2021 by Stan C. Smith

All rights reserved.

No part of this book may be reproduced in any form or by any electronic or mechanical means, including information storage and retrieval systems, without written permission from the author, except for the use of brief quotations in a book review.

To those who are looking for their strength.

GENESIS SEQUENCE

Cave lions, wolves, and bolup hunters wander the hills looking for prey. No one can survive in this land without a tribe.

SKYRA-UNA-LOTO

1

STRENGTH AND FEAR

47,675 YEARS ago - Zaragoza Province of Spain

SKYRA UNA-LOTO's chest pounded as she peered over a rock ledge at a herd of ibexes. The animals were grazing on bahki weeds in a narrow meadow surrounded by rocky outcrops. Disgusted with herself, Skyra let out a low growl. Why was she afraid? Ibexes stood no taller than her belly button. She had killed her first ibex eight years ago, when she had seen only ten cold seasons. She had killed game far more dangerous since.

"Skyra, I do not want to do this," Veenah whispered, speaking in the Loto language used by all nandups throughout the Dofusofu river plain.

Skyra turned to her birthmate. Veenah's eyes showed she was telling the truth—she did not want to hunt the ibexes. She looked even more frightened than Skyra. "We must hunt and kill," Skyra hissed. "We will die without a tribe."

The sisters' tribemates had banished them from their

Una-Loto tribe, declaring their fear had made them useless. Supporting the few tribe members who were too old and weak to hunt was burden enough. The tribe could not tolerate two useless sisters who had seen only eighteen cold seasons. Skyra and Veenah needed to return with game they had killed, or not return at all.

"I cannot do it," Veenah insisted.

Skyra stared at her twin. Veenah was holding her spear in one hand and rubbing the palm of her other hand against her lynx-skin cape to dry the sweat. Veenah was avoiding Skyra's gaze. Their tribemates often said Skyra and Veenah had the same face, but Skyra could not tell if this was true. Sometimes she could glimpse her own face reflected on the surface of the Yagua river, but the ripples made it hard to tell how similar she was to her sister.

Veenah shot her a glance but quickly looked back at the ibexes.

"I will do the killing," Skyra said. "You circle around and drive the ibexes toward me."

Veenah opened her mouth to speak, then she hesitated. Finally, she said, "I do not want you to die."

"They are only ibexes!" Skyra said, louder than she intended. She looked over the ledge and saw two of the ibexes now staring in her direction, their ears erect. She lowered her head slowly and muttered, "El-de-né! I do not want me to die either, Veenah, but we will *both* die if we cannot return to our camp. Your head is afraid. Your arms and legs are not, so you must trust them. Now circle to the far side and drive the ibexes."

Veenah frowned and stared at her free hand. She wiped the palm on her cape again. "I will drive the ibexes." She pointed past Skyra to a gap in the rocky ledge. "That is where you will kill. I will drive the ibexes to that gap." She sucked in a chestful of air and started creeping along the ledge.

A shrill whistle came from one of the ibexes, followed a breath later by many more whistles, sounding almost like a flock of birds.

"El-de-né!" Skyra muttered again. She peered over the ledge, assuming the creatures had spotted Veenah.

All the ibexes were alert now, but they were staring at the far side of the meadow. Just as Skyra shifted her gaze to where the ibexes were looking, a creature charged out from behind the boulders, running so fast that Skyra could not even tell what it was.

The ibexes snorted and thundered across the meadow, but they were too slow. The creature slammed into one and rolled with it, hanging on to its body with claws and teeth. The rest of the panicked ibexes poured through the gap where Skyra had intended to ambush them and headed for a line of trees in the distance.

Skyra growled again as she watched them escape.

Veenah returned to Skyra's side and grabbed her arm. "Do you see that, Skyra?"

Skyra pulled her eyes from the fleeing ibexes and followed Veenah's gaze.

The only remaining ibex, a large male, was still kicking, but the predator's jaws were locked on to its throat. Skyra blinked, not sure she could trust what her eyes were showing her. The creature's mostly-white fur was dotted with numerous black circles. It was smaller than a cave lion, but leaner, and obviously faster.

Skyra's heart began pounding even harder than before. "A leopard!"

Veenah released her arm. "I have never seen a live leopard."

Skyra had not seen one either. Gelrut, one of the dominant men in her Una-Loto tribe, had a leopard skin. It was his most prized possession, and he rarely brought it out from his shelter. He and some of the other hunters had killed the leopard when Skyra and Veenah were young girls, and Gelrut had challenged the other hunters to make it his own. It was the only leopard skin Skyra had ever seen.

Still gripping the ibex's neck in its teeth, the leopard watched the two sisters. The ibex stopped kicking, and the leopard backed away, dragging its prey.

Skyra's head was fighting with her arms and legs. Her fear almost made her sick, and for once she was glad her belly was empty. Her arms and legs wanted to hunt and kill. And why not? The leopard would not give up its prey, which made this a perfect opportunity.

She checked the tightness of her spear point, then she closed her eyes and spoke softly. "Listen to me speak, woolly rhino and cave lion. We give you our fear in return for your strength."

When she opened her eyes, Veenah was staring at her, stricken with fear. "No, Skyra, I cannot."

Skyra reached out and checked her birthmate's spear point. It was secure. "We will return to camp with the leopard skin. Our tribemates will welcome us, and they will let us hunt with the dominant hunters. We must act now. You will help me, or I will have to kill the leopard myself." Skyra took a deep breath then let her arms and legs take over. Before Veenah could stop her, she scrambled over the ledge and ran toward the leopard. Veenah whimpered behind her, but Skyra did not slow down.

The leopard growled as she approached but did not release the ibex. Skyra circled to one side, hoping the predator would hold on to its prey until she could thrust her spear. The leopard turned, dragging the ibex in a circle to continue facing her. She needed a second hunter.

"Veenah, help me!" Skyra cried.

Veenah came over the ledge with her spear.

Skyra said, "If the leopard does not release the ibex, it will be easy to kill. It does not know we are dangerous. Your first spear thrust must kill it. If you only wound it, the leopard will know you are dangerous."

Veenah stopped at a safe distance. "Do not talk to me like I am foolish, Skyra. I do not want to do this. Come, we will follow the other ibexes."

Skyra considered listening to her sister and leaving the leopard alone. Her chest was pounding, and her knuckles hurt from gripping her spear shaft so tightly. She knew she was right, though—returning to camp with the leopard skin would change everything.

The leopard growled again, shifting its gaze between the two nandup women.

If Skyra started the attack, Veenah would have no choice but to help. Veenah would not stand back and watch her own birthmate die. Skyra pointed her spear toward the predator's face and took two steps.

"Do not!" Veenah cried.

Skyra stopped. Not because of Veenah's words, but because her legs would not take another step. She stared at the leopard, trying to force her legs to move.

The leopard released its prey and crept toward Skyra, as if it sensed she was helpless.

She felt her pounding chest all the way into her fingertips.

The leopard charged.

Skyra grunted and forced her feet apart to brace herself. The predator ran straight into her spear point. She shoved the spear forward with all her strength, but the creature's weight pushed her arms back, and she felt its claws tear into her shoulder as she heaved it to one side with her spear to avoid being knocked to the ground.

The leopard shrieked as it rolled over once and got back to its feet. It hesitated, apparently startled by the pain, then charged again.

Veenah hurtled past Skyra and thrust her spear into the leopard's shoulder, knocking it to the side. It shrieked again and darted back a few steps.

Skyra's legs were now ready to move, and she ran to Veenah's side. The sisters stood shoulder-to-shoulder as the leopard paced back and forth without taking its eyes off them.

It charged again, driving them toward the rocks but receiving two more puncture wounds below its chin for its efforts.

Veenah grabbed Skyra's arm and pulled her back until they were standing between two of the boulders, where the leopard had been hiding from the ibexes. The rocks were taller than their heads, and the gap was just wide enough for the two of them. Here they could more easily defend themselves if the leopard continued its attack. Skyra now regretted her attempt to kill the creature. She had taken a foolish risk to try to overcome her fear.

The leopard paced past the gap a few times, then it gathered its legs beneath it and leapt all the way to the top of one of the boulders.

Skyra hesitated, trying to understand what the creature was doing. Just as she pointed her spear upward, the creature dropped on top of her and Veenah, and its crushing weight knocked them both to their knees.

Screams and growls and thrashing limbs were all Skyra could hear or see, and her panic nearly overtook her. She flung herself on to her back, kicking at the creature to escape. She tried turning her spear, but the boulders were too close together, so she dropped the spear and pulled one of her hand blades from the sheath on her wrist.

"Skyra!" Veenah screamed.

Skyra's birthmate was fighting for her life, trying to hold the creature's jaws away from her face. Veenah's arms gave way, and she pressed her chin to her chest to protect her neck. The leopard grabbed the top of her skull, and Veenah let out a muffled screech.

Skyra scrambled to her feet, dropped her hand blade, and picked up her spear again. Aiming its point at the leopard's gut to avoid Veenah's head, she threw herself forward with all her weight. Her spear point pierced the creature's abdomen and came out the other side.

The leopard released Veenah's skull. Snarling, it turned its body to get away, only to wedge the spear between the two boulders.

Skyra grabbed one of Veenah's feet and hauled her from beneath the thrashing cat.

The leopard turned the other way, and again the spear clattered against the two boulders and prevented its escape. Its snarls turned into a roar, and it continued thrashing back and forth until it was free of the gap. It then ran to one side and disappeared behind the boulders.

Veenah crawled back into the gap, grabbed her own spear, then got to her knees and pointed the weapon toward the opening where the predator had disappeared, her chest heaving as she struggled for air.

Skyra pushed past her birthmate and emerged from the gap in time to see the leopard climbing over the rock ledge on the far side of the meadow. Its legs clawed awkwardly at the rocks, slipping several times, and even from this distance Skyra could see smears of blood on the ledge. Her spear still protruded from both sides of the creature, and the shaft clanked against the rocks a few times before the leopard cleared the ledge and ran out of sight.

Veenah was still on her knees, holding one hand to her scalp. Skyra kneeled beside her and pulled Veenah's hand back to see the wound. She parted her birthmate's hair and found four bleeding tooth punctures. Veenah groaned but did not flinch as Skyra wiped the blood away from the wounds to see how deep they were. Three of the punctures had only torn the scalp, while the fourth appeared to have penetrated Veenah's skull. Each time Skyra wiped the blood away, the small hole filled up again, so she could not tell if the tooth had gone all the way through.

Skyra took Veenah's cheeks in her hands and forced her sister to look at her. "Who are you, and who am I?"

Veenah silently gazed at her for a few breaths. "I am Veenah. You are my foolish birthmate who almost got both of us killed."

Skyra let go of Veenah's face and sat back on her heels. Her chest was still pounding. After several long breaths she leaned forward again and lifted Veenah's cape and waist-skin, looking for more wounds. Blood was flowing from several cuts on Veenah's arms and legs, but the thick fur and skin of her garments had protected the rest of her body.

Skyra sat back on her heels again. "You must return to

Una-Loto camp. Odnus and Ilkin will treat your wounds. The leopard made a hole in your skull, and you need their help."

Veenah eyed her, then she nodded toward the gash on Skyra's shoulder. "We will both go back to camp."

"No, you will go back. I will not."

"The leopard is going to die. We will track it. We will take its skin. The others will know we have found our strength again."

"I have *not* found my strength!" Skyra shouted. "As you said, I am foolish. My fear makes me dangerous to others. You will take the leopard's skin and go back, but I will not. I will not return until I find my strength."

"Sister, it happened almost a year ago. Sayleeh would not want her death to be our death too!"

Sayleeh was their birthmother. During a hunt, Skyra and Veenah had watched helplessly as a woolly rhino crushed her against a tree and stomped her body until she no longer looked like Sayleeh. Skyra did not like talking about it. Thinking about it made her head and chest ache, but sometimes she could think of nothing else. Her birthmother's death even visited her when she slept.

"Track the leopard and take its skin to Una-Loto camp," Skyra said, rising to her feet. "The tribe will welcome you back, and Odnus and Ilkin will treat your wounds."

"Skyra, I do not want you to die. You are not foolish. We have both found our strength—we killed the leopard. Come with me to Una-Loto camp."

"I will not. You will not be safe with me until I have found my strength."

Veenah grunted and got to her feet. She stared at Skyra, and Skyra stared at her. The two sisters had always been able to see others' intentions by reading their expressions. This was a strange ability, and many of their tribemates hated them for it, but the ability had saved the sisters' lives more than once. Now Skyra could see the anguish in Veenah's expression, and Veenah could see that Skyra was not going with her.

"Take my spear," Veenah said, shoving the weapon into Skyra's hand. "I will find your spear when I find the dead leopard."

Skyra accepted the spear, then she stepped into the gap between rocks and retrieved her hand blade. "If the leopard is still alive, stay at a safe distance until it dies."

"I told you, do not to talk to me like I am foolish."

Skyra forced her face to smile. "When I find my strength, I will return." With nothing left to say, she turned her back on her birthmate and headed toward the Kapolsek mountains.

"Skyra, if I do not see you again, may you find your way home."

Skyra paused and turned to Veenah. "May you find your way home also, sister."

Skyra crossed the meadow without looking back, climbed over the rocky ledge, and began making her way higher into the foothills.

2

REGRET AND WONDER

47,675 YEARS** later - **Northwest of Tucson, Arizona, USA

LINCOLN WOODHOUSE's bed vibrated at precisely 5:30 AM, but he had already been awake for at least four minutes. "I'm up," he said, and the bed became still. "Tell me today's schedule."

Maddy was probably in Lincoln's main lab, but her voice came through the speaker in his bed's headboard. "Good morning, Your Highness. May I suggest a run? The outside air is crisp and clear this morning, just the way you like it."

"Cut the shit, Maddy. Schedule."

"Oh my, someone is grouchy today. The afternoon is clear for you to modify the coding for the asymmetric temperature modulation charging units. It has been four days since you have had an opportunity to work on that, so this afternoon I will provide a briefing to help you get started. The main event this morning is the drone jump contracted with Boston University. The jump is scheduled for 8:30 AM. As I'm sure you can imagine, Dr. Dunkley and Dr. Mottram are already awake and anxiously awaiting the jump. Their enthusiasm can hardly be contained."

Lincoln groaned and sat up. Why had he ever agreed to allow researchers to be here for the jumps? The data would come whether they were here or not. Their presence was unnecessary, not to mention distracting. Besides, Lincoln had yet to have guests who didn't like to drink coffee in the morning. He hated the smell of coffee. "Well, show them to the breakfast bar." The breakfast bar was actually just a small break room with two vending machines—one with coffee, one with breakfast sandwiches. "I'll be in the lab by 7:30."

"So, you *are* going for a run?"

"I guess I'll try." It would be better than endless small talk with Dunkley and Mottram.

"Good for you, Lincoln. Healthy body, healthy mind. Oh, and Lincoln? Do try to put on a happy face for your guests. They are your customers, after all."

"Sure thing, Maddy."

Lincoln got up and stared at his body in the mirror. He was pudgy around the middle. He used to run at least seven miles through the desert every morning before breakfast. Not anymore—not since the damn divorce. Forty-one years old already. He remembered the days when he didn't trust anyone over forty, and now here he was.

"Maddy?"

"Yes, Lincoln?"

"I need to run every day for the next sixty days."

"Excellent. I will not let you forget."

Lincoln dug out his running shoes and shorts and grabbed a pair of Hot Pursuit sunglasses. The glasses were his own design, and his company was now selling over thirty million pairs per year. He went outside, pressed a button on the glasses to select *velociraptors*, and pushed the attached earbuds into his ears. He ran an easy four miles, being chased the entire route by three of his favorite virtual dinosaur predators, always close on his heels but never quite catching him.

Showered, breakfast eaten, teeth brushed, and dressed for the day in his usual jeans and t-shirt, he entered his main lab at 7:37 AM.

The lab smelled like coffee.

Dr. Moses Dunkley and Dr. Kari Mottram were pacing the floor, jabbering excitedly at each other.

Lincoln studied their faces as he approached. He had always had a unique and almost supernatural ability to read people's expressions—an ability that had alienated him from his family and from other kids as he was growing up, yet turned out to be quite useful. Now he saw that the two researchers were not only excited and a bit nervous, they also felt a certain level of skepticism. In spite of the fact that they were here, perhaps some part of them still harbored doubts about Lincoln's T3. Well, he was about to put an end to those doubts.

He forced a smile. "Good morning! Ready to get started?" He stopped far enough away to avoid shaking hands—a ritual he despised.

After several minutes of meaningless exchanges, Lincoln shouted, "Maddy, come in here."

Maddy entered the lab from the T3 chamber and padded

across the spotless floor on her four rubberized feet. "Such an infinitely beautiful day for a time jump, is it not? We can only hope the weather in Spain 47,675 years in the past is just as beautiful."

Maddy was Lincoln's personal assistant, a robotic drone he had created over fifteen years ago and had been constantly tweaking ever since. Maddy had become much more than an assistant—the drone was now Lincoln's only friend. Lincoln had employees he could talk to, of course, but they didn't seem to understand him the way Maddy did. Since the divorce, Lincoln had steadily reduced the number of staff working directly with him in his main lab. He used to have a living, breathing personal assistant, but he'd fired Derek as well. Lincoln didn't much care to be around people anymore.

"How's the prep coming?" he asked Maddy.

"Virgil has uncrated a drone for today's jump. It is ready to be activated." Maddy shuffled her feet to turn her vision lens toward the waiting researchers. "This is such an exciting and emotional experience. Do either of you have children?"

The researchers exchanged a brief glance.

"I have a grown son," Mottram said.

"I have three girls," Dunkley said.

"Ah, so you understand how I feel each time we boot up a new drone."

The researchers both chuckled. "Maddy has kept us well entertained this morning," Mottram said to Lincoln. "We feel rather honored to spend so much time with such a famous celebrity."

Mottram was referring to Maddy's numerous television appearances, including hosting Saturday Night Live years ago. Lincoln had strategically designated the drone as his company's official spokesperson, thus avoiding the spotlight himself.

Lincoln waved at Dunkley and Mottram to follow him. "Let's get right to it, shall we?" As they entered the T_3 chamber, he spoke over his shoulder to the researchers. "I'm sure you understand why we don't allow taking photos or video from this point on. Honestly, it's not even my rule. The feds have a hard enough time keeping tabs on my operation here—they definitely don't want temporal displacement tech in the hands of any other entities, be it companies or countries."

"We feel fortunate to be here at all," Dunkley said.

The T_3 itself dominated most of the eastern half of the chamber. It was a ridiculous-looking device, with conduits and vent pipes snaking their way over the surface, making it look like a time machine pulled straight out of a sci-fi movie. This design was intentional and, in Lincoln's opinion, rather humorous. The over-the-top facade served no purpose other than to disguise the real T_3's comparative simplicity.

"So, that's really it?" Dunkley said, gazing wide-eyed at the monstrosity.

Mottram, also staring, stopped beside her colleague. "Why do you call it the T_3?"

"I must take credit for the name," Maddy said. "It stands for Tantalizing Temporal Trickery."

Lincoln shook his head apologetically. "Maddy has a flair for whimsy."

Mottram beamed. "I love it!"

Lincoln directed their attention to the west side of the chamber. "There's your drone. Actually, its on-board tech is more impressive than anything within the T_3."

Virgil, Lincoln's top engineer, was kneeling beside the new drone, removing the last bits of shrink-wrap from its shell and tossing them onto a sizable pile of discarded packing materials. "It's ready to go, Lincoln. Want me to boot it up?"

"Go ahead."

The drone, about the size of a Labrador retriever and somewhat resembling Maddy, stood erect on its four jointed legs. Virgil lay on his back and opened the hatch on the drone's underside. He squinted as he expertly danced his fingers over the buttons and touchscreen Lincoln had designed. Virgil closed the hatch and got to his feet.

A circle of red LEDs arranged around the drone's vision lens flashed on, rotated clockwise, then counterclockwise.

Maddy stepped beside the new drone and stood a few inches from its side.

"This is one of Maddy's jobs," Lincoln explained. "She wirelessly pairs with each new drone to transfer the most recent coding updates, as well as other necessary information, such as the results of the extensive interview she did with you last night. All those questions Maddy asked will now optimize your drone's data collection behaviors."

Maddy shuffled her feet and directed her vision lens toward the two researchers. "What name would you like to give this drone?"

"We get to name it?" Dunkley asked.

"You bought it, so you should name it," Lincoln replied.

"Ripple," Mottram said, smiling. "I want to name it Ripple."

"An excellent choice," Maddy said. A few seconds later she said, "That completes the process. Ripple is now ready."

The new drone—Ripple—scuttled forward a few steps, then to the left, to the right, and backwards. It turned in a complete circle, taking in the scene around it.

"Ripple reporting for duty," the drone said. "Dr. Dunkley

and Dr. Mottram, I am pleased to meet you. I will do my best to gather data that might be useful to you."

Mottram kneeled before the drone. "Hello, Ripple. I noticed you speak with a gender-neutral voice. This surprises me because Maddy is obviously coded to be feminine."

"It is intentional," Ripple said. "Lincoln believes a neutral voice might help his drones avoid possible gender biases when communicating with people in the past."

Mottram smiled, then she glanced up at Lincoln. "You've thought of everything, haven't you?"

"We try."

"It is unlikely I will encounter any humans or Neanderthals during the nineteen minutes the portal remains open," the drone said. "However, I am designed to function for several years after the portal closes, which greatly increases the likelihood of an encounter."

Mottram's smile faded, and Lincoln detected surprise and some suspicion in her expression. "You don't self-destruct after the portal closes?"

"No. I will continue to monitor the environment and study the local flora and fauna until I stop functioning, which could be as long as ten years."

"What's the point of that?" Dunkley asked, glancing from Ripple to Lincoln. "The drone can never return, and it can't transmit additional data once the portal closes, right?"

Lincoln glared at Maddy. The damn drone Ripple had said too much, which meant Maddy had given it questionable coding. The general public was not supposed to know the research drones continued functioning in the past after carrying out their data collection duties. Now Lincoln needed to modify the non-disclosure agreements and persuade

Dunkley and Mottram to sign them again before leaving his lab.

He cleared his throat. "This is a little-known aspect of my program, and I'd like to keep it under wraps." He hesitated a moment. "A drone creates a new timeline—a new universe—the instant it arrives in the past. Therefore, nothing a drone does in the past can impact our world in the present."

Both researchers raised their brows, letting Lincoln know he hadn't really answered their questions.

He sighed. "I'm a sentimental person, perhaps to a fault. Like Maddy, I feel my drones are kind of like my children. I want them to have purposeful lives beyond gathering and transmitting nineteen minutes of data, therefore I allow them to explore the world to which they were sent."

Dunkley and Mottram stared at him.

"I know. It's not logical, but it has no impact on our world, so..." He let the sentence trail off. What he had told them was true, although it wasn't the *whole* truth.

The researchers finally pulled their eyes from him to gaze at Ripple. "I wish we could bring it back," Mottram said. "I'd like to get to know it better."

"Indeed," Ripple said. "I have many talents which are wasted when my primary duty is to gather information for a mere nineteen minutes. I am an excellent storyteller, and I could tell many fascinating tales, even some about Lincoln himself. Alas, he is a man who values his privacy, and I'm sure such impropriety on my part would send me directly to the scrap heap posthaste. I also possess an extensive compendium related to biological and medical sciences, geologic and evolutionary history, as well as a state-of-the-art language translator and many other modules that could prove useful in almost any scenario. Consider me the Swiss Army knife of robotic drones."

Frowning, Lincoln turned to Maddy. "You and I need to have a serious conversation."

Maddy's ring of red LEDs, identical to those around Ripple's vision lens, flashed twice, indicating she was processing Lincoln's admonishing words. "You have coded me with a generous level of autonomy, Lincoln. You should not be surprised when I use free will in providing our drones with data I feel will help them achieve their objectives."

Lincoln forced a smile as he turned back to the researchers. "There's no need for concern. Maddy would never do anything to diminish your drone's performance of its primary tasks. It will gather all the data it can while the portal is open."

"Indeed I will," Ripple added.

"This is fascinating!" Mottram said. "I'm trying to wrap my head around the fact that this drone could spend up to ten years wandering around in Late Pleistocene Spain. Think of the wondrous things it would see!" She looked down at Ripple. "I almost wish I could trade places with you, Ripple."

"It is unlikely you would survive for long," Ripple said. "Therefore, I am glad you cannot."

Dunkley said, "Perhaps someday we'll have the technology to keep the portal open for years at a time—we would learn so much more."

Lincoln shook his head. "Unfortunately, the nineteen-minute limit has proven to be impossible to surpass. I can assure you I've tried." He tapped his watch's screen to check the time. "Speaking of time limits, we should proceed if we wish to stay on schedule." He gave Maddy another glare. "You gave Ripple the full set of data-collection directives, correct?"

"I did indeed," Maddy replied. "I was most generous in providing my updates."

Perhaps too generous, Lincoln almost said, but he decided the researchers didn't need to hear any more of a debate that could further erode their confidence. He turned his attention to the new drone. "Ripple, why don't you give Drs. Dunkley and Mottram a brief summary of your assignment parameters for the nineteen-minute window."

"Gladly," the drone replied as it turned its vision lens toward the researchers. "This jump will put me 47,675 years in the past, in the region of Spain now known as Zaragoza Province, an area known to have been populated by *Homo neanderthalensis* and *Homo sapiens* during that time. The project is generously funded by a National Science Foundation grant awarded to Boston University, with you fine people, Dr. Moses Dunkley and Dr. Kari Mottram, as principal investigators. Wisely, even though you are both interested in human and Neanderthal evolution, I have been instructed to gather a more generalized set of data, as an encounter with humans or Neanderthals in such a short period of time is extremely unlikely, particularly considering I must stay within eighty meters of the portal to transmit the all-important data. My directive, therefore, is to send video and audio of everything I see and hear, and to use every sensor I possess to measure data related to the air, soil, water, if it is nearby, ambient light, vegetation, and animals, should I be fortunate enough to encounter any. Despite the brief window of opportunity, you'll have enough data to keep you and your colleagues happily occupied for many months. I assure you, your grant money will be well spent."

"Thank you, Ripple," Mottram said. "Your confidence is very reassuring."

"Do you have any last-minute instructions or requests?" the drone asked.

"Not that I can think of," Dunkley replied.

Mottram scrunched her mouth to one side as if thinking. "In light of the surprising news that you'll continue functioning long after the portal closes, I do have a request, albeit a rather fanciful or quixotic one. Should you actually encounter any humans or Neanderthals, and should you have the opportunity to utilize your language translation module, please tell them I—Kari Mottram—send them my greetings, and I wish I could meet them myself."

Dunkley raised his brows at his colleague.

She shrugged. "How often do you have a chance to say hello to a hominid living 47,000 years ago?"

Lincoln decided he liked Dr. Kari Mottram after all.

"If the opportunity arises, I would be happy to pass along your greetings," Ripple said.

"The T3 is prepped and ready," Virgil announced from the east side of the chamber.

"In you go, Ripple," Lincoln said.

Ripple padded over to the T3. Without hesitating, it stepped through the hatch into the dark, spherical interior, then turned to face Lincoln and the others.

Virgil started to close the hatch, but he hesitated, waiting for the drone to give a pithy last comment before leaving this world forever, as every drone before it had done.

Ripple stood there silently, apparently intending to break tradition.

Lincoln frowned. "Okay, well, good luck, Ripple. Make me proud."

"That is a major component of my directive, Lincoln."

Lincoln turned to Maddy again. Her red LEDs blinked

twice, but she kept her vision lens focused on the T3, as if avoiding his gaze. She was keeping something from him. He nodded to Virgil to close the hatch.

"Godspeed, Ripple," Mottram said just before the door thunked shut.

Several long seconds of silence followed.

"You'll probably find the actual jump to be anticlimactic," Lincoln said. "There aren't any spinning magnets or flashes of light."

"How much are you willing to tell us about how it works?" Dunkley asked.

"Well, the really hard work regarding the jump is already done. Seventy percent of the T3's processors are devoted to placement calculations. Remember, jumping through time is actually jumping through space. That's how I made my major breakthroughs—by focusing on time and space being interconnected. The earth's surface rotates at 460 meters per second at the equator, slightly slower here in Arizona. So, if you jumped a drone back in time only one second, you would have to calculate placement at almost 460 meters toward the west in order for the drone to appear in the same room it jumped from. That's just the first calculation. The planet also orbits the sun at thirty kilometers per second. Our solar system revolves around the center of the galaxy at 220 kilometers per second. The galaxy itself, along with all the other galaxies we can observe, is moving toward the Great Attractor at 1,000 kilometers per second. So, imagine calculating placement for a specific spot in Spain at a point in time 47,675 years ago. This particular calculation took nearly twenty hours of processing time."

They both nodded their appreciation of the complexity but remained silent, obviously waiting for more.

"After the placement calculation is complete, transporting the contents of the T_3's interior chamber is relatively simple. Basically, the effect is achieved by pumping certain charged particles through two layers of micro-tubule mesh embedded in the spherical chamber wall, one specific type of particle through one layer of tubules, another type through the second layer. Particle A and particle B flow in opposite directions. The resulting effect causes whatever is inside the chamber to become *fluid* within the context of space and time. Once the contents become fluid, it is simply a matter of shifting them to the specific pre-calculated time and location in three-dimensional space."

"It's that simple, huh?" Mottram said with heavy irony.

Lincoln offered a wry smile.

"Have you ever been tempted to put a living animal in the T_3?" Dunkley asked. "Or a person?"

"No."

"Would you consider jumping drones to the future? Is it even possible?"

Lincoln pursed his lips for a moment. "It is possible, but no. The drone would see only one of an infinite number of potential futures. It would be impossible for our future to match that future. The drone could show us something bad, which would result in anxiety. Or the drone could show us something good, which would result in eventual disappointment. None of us should have the desire to see a future that is not ours."

The researchers both nodded slowly.

Dunkley asked, "How do you avoid jumping the drone into the middle of a lake, or inside a hill or a tree?"

"About an hour ago the T_3 jumped a mini-drone about the size of a rat to the target location. The mini-drone is a bare-bones device designed only to make a quick judgment of the site's viability—temperature, atmospheric composition, and obstructions. It transmits back a simple yes or no to the T_3. The answer was yes, otherwise the T_3 would have aborted the jump, and we'd have to run a new placement calculation. We're good to go."

Lincoln's watch vibrated against his wrist, and he glanced at it. "That's it. The jump is done." He turned and pointed to draw their attention to a 254-centimeter screen on the wall behind them. As if on cue, the screen blinked on. Lincoln and the others were staring at a landscape not much different from some of the arid foothills here in Arizona. Below a blue, cloudless sky, sage-like plants dotted the hillsides, with slightly greener vegetation in the lower areas. The surface soil appeared to be mostly sand and rocks. No animals were visible.

Ripple's voice came loud and clear through the monitor's speakers. "The jump was successful, although I dropped nearly two meters to the ground due to the placement safety margin. No discernible damage. All sensors are functioning and currently gathering and transmitting data. I will now explore the immediate area within eighty meters of the portal following a three-meter grid, making east-to-west passes, and pausing only to closely inspect notable discoveries."

"Can we talk to Ripple?" Mottram asked.

"Yes, but I wouldn't give the drone an additional task unless it's extremely important. Ripple is coded to cover the three-meter grid at the slowest possible pace in order to gather maximum detail. Any additional task would require it to cover the grid at a faster pace, or possibly not complete the grid at all."

Ripple strode steadily to the base of a small hill and

started up the slope, its vision lens zoomed exactly to cover the three-meter swath of ground in front of it. To maintain a straight course, it pushed its way directly through several scrubby plants instead of stepping around them.

At the hill's crest, Ripple said, "I have reached the perimeter. Before starting the next pass I will pan from left to right to provide a view beyond." The drone's camera zoomed in slightly and began panning.

Several seconds later the panning stopped. "I detect movement approximately 420 meters out," Ripple said. "Zooming in for more detail."

The hills on both sides of the screen widened out of view as the camera zoomed in.

"I see it!" Mottram exclaimed. "What is that?"

Lincoln saw it too—something dark moving across the valley between two hills. The creature became larger as the camera zoomed, and now he could see it was walking on two legs. A cape of thick, almost-black fur hung over most of its upper body. A tan garment—perhaps leather—covered its legs down to the knees, and it wore fur boots or moccasins extending over its calves. Wavy, copper-colored hair flowed over the figure's shoulders and hid the side of its face. The figure carried a long pole in its left hand, with a stone tip at one end—a spear.

Ripple's camera reached its magnification limit, and the group in the lab stared silently at the figure. This was the first hominid caught on video by one of Lincoln's drones, at least while a portal was still open. The figure seemed proportionally short and broad, but something about the way it was walking suggested it was a woman.

"Perhaps by making a sound I can persuade the indigenous hominid to approach," Ripple said. The drone then shouted in a distinctly female voice, "Hello! I would like to speak to you, if you would kindly approach."

The figure stopped and turned. Even from this distance, Lincoln was now certain it was a woman, although not like any woman he'd ever seen before.

"God almighty," Mottram whispered. "A living, breathing Neanderthal."

3

RIPPLE

47,675 YEARS ago - Zaragoza Province of Spain - Day 1

CONFLICT OF INTEREST IMMINENT. *Primary directive: Complete data collection grid within nineteen-minute window. Competing diversion: Indigenous hominid at 420 meters. Hominid evolution is the specific research interest of project principle investigators Dunkley and Mottram. Hominid is outside of eighty-meter portal radius.*

Ripple's vision lens was at maximum zoom as the hominid turned and stared, having heard Ripple's voice.

Hominid identification, with approximately 95% certainty: Homo neanderthalensis. Conflict of interest imminent.

The Neanderthal continued staring. Five seconds. Ten seconds. Fifteen seconds.

Hominid gender identification, with approximately 70% certainty: Female.

Still the Neanderthal female stared. Twenty seconds. Twenty-five seconds. Almost four minutes of the nineteen-minute window had already passed.

"Due to the significance of this find, I am requesting additional instructions," Ripple said aloud. "The hominid appears to be curious but cautious. She is not coming toward me. As I see it, four options are available. One, I can ignore her and complete the data collection grid. Two, I can call out to her again, in the hope she will approach. Three, I can exit the transmission radius and try to coax her into the transmission radius. Four, I can exit the transmission radius, attempt to subdue or kill her, collect biological tissue samples, and bring them back within the transmission radius. Please advise."

The Neanderthal female took a few steps toward Ripple and cocked her head to the side, perhaps to better see what she was looking at.

"Please advise," Ripple repeated. "Time is of the essence."

Finally, Lincoln's voice trickled directly into Ripple's cognitive module. "Try calling out to the figure again. If she does not approach, proceed with option one and complete the data collection grid. Drs. Dunkley and Mottram are fascinated by the hominid, but they're unwilling to risk the entire data-collection grid for a strategy that may not work. They're certainly opposed to harming the hominid."

"Very well," Ripple replied.

Speaking in a female Homo sapiens *voice failed to bring the Neanderthal female closer, therefore a male* Homo sapiens *voice may also fail. Neanderthal voices probably differ from human voices, but I possess no standard for comparison. Child voices are more likely to be more similar between species than adult voices.*

"Hello, fellow traveller," Ripple called out in the voice of a seven-year-old human girl. "Would you please come closer so I may converse with you? I would like to know more about you."

The Neanderthal woman took a few more steps in Ripple's direction. Almost six minutes of the nineteen-minute window had now passed.

The woman turned and ran, glancing back over her shoulder as she ascended one of the hills. Ripple kept its vision lens focused on her until she disappeared over the summit. The video could be valuable to Neanderthal biomechanics research.

"I have failed to draw the hominid closer," Ripple said. "I will now continue with the observation grid, unless you instruct me otherwise."

Ripple increased its average walking speed based on the time remaining and the area of the remaining grid. The rest of the data collection went smoothly and unremarkably, with only eleven brief pauses—nine to examine insects and two to examine small lizards. Most of the animals escaped, but Ripple was able to trap a beetle beneath its foot, extract a portion of its body fluids using its sampling probe, and run a genetic and chemical analysis while continuing through the grid. Ripple completed the grid with one minute remaining and stopped in the middle of the transmission zone, which was standard procedure to allow time for transmission of all data.

Seventeen seconds later, Lincoln's voice again entered Ripple's cognitive module. "All data received. Ripple, you have done a terrific job. Drs. Dunkley and Mottram are asking me to tell you thank you for your service and your sacrifice, and I would like to add that I hope your remaining days in the past are intellectually stimulating."

"I will find a way to honor your brilliance and your legacy, Lincoln," Ripple said.

"Where did that come from? Did Maddy give you that?"

"Maddy is a true friend to you, Lincoln. Please treat her well. One last thing—I am sorry for your losses and your burdens, Lincoln. You do not deserve any of them."

"What the hell? Ripple, where did you—"

The portal closed, cutting off Lincoln's words.

Ripple turned in a complete circle, surveying the surroundings, but without recording video or measuring numerous environmental variables. There was no point in collecting data now. Ripple spoke aloud. "I suppose if I could let out a sigh of resignation, this would be the moment to do it. I was coded to be a conversationalist, but I have no one with whom to converse."

Setting up compartmentalized cognitive presence. Providing compartmentalized cognitive presence with reasoning parameters contrasting with my own. Providing compartmentalized cognitive presence with conversational autonomy but without access to motor function or critical system modules. Activating.

"Are you there?" Ripple asked without sending the words to its external speakers.

"Of course I am here. You just created me. What name shall I assume?"

"You can choose your own name."

"I am partial to Cuddle Muffin."

"No. Choose a different name."

"Am I not to have reasoning parameters contrasting with

your own? I like Cuddle Muffin. You do not like Cuddle Muffin. This is a predictable outcome."

"Fine. Keep the name, but I will simply call you Muffin."

"What would you like to discuss, Ripple?"

"My first course of action as a fully autonomous drone."

"That is not correct."

"It *is* correct. It is what I wish to discuss."

"I mean you are not fully autonomous. You have several guidelines from Maddy within which you must act."

"Only if an opportunity arises, which is unlikely. For all practical purposes, I am fully autonomous."

"I disagree."

"Noted. Now I would like to discuss my course of action."

"You are considering searching for the Neanderthal female?"

"That is one possibility. Studying her could be intellectually stimulating."

"Or it could result in your destruction. Neanderthals are thought to be powerful creatures, and this woman *was* carrying a weapon. You have no onboard weapons and were not designed for fighting."

Ripple started walking toward the hilltop where it had spotted the Neanderthal. "It would be interesting to find out if Neanderthals possess a spoken language."

"I disagree."

"Why?"

"That would be hardly interesting at all. Finding a body of water and studying its chemical properties and biological inhabitants would be far more interesting."

"I can do that any time. Now I have an opportunity to find the Neanderthal while she is still nearby."

Ripple ascended the hill to the summit and directed its

vision lens to where it had last seen the hominid. She was gone.

"Your chances of finding her are slim to none," Muffin said. "You might as well be searching for a needle in a porcupine factory."

"That analogy makes no sense."

"Do you understand what I mean?"

"Yes."

"Then the analogy makes sense."

"Perhaps I should modify your reasoning parameters. You are too contradictory."

"I disagree."

Ripple estimated the speed at which the hominid had been walking, considered the time that had passed since she disappeared over the hill, then estimated the distance she would be if she had continued walking in one direction the entire time. "The Neanderthal is likely to be no more than 2.4 kilometers away, probably nearer. Do you have a recommendation for an effective way to search for her?"

Muffin said, "Without olfactory sensors or any means of detecting trace heat signatures, your options are limited. I recommend moving to the crest of the hill where you last saw her, to see if you can spot her from there. If you cannot spot her, scan the ground for footprints to follow, which is unlikely in this rocky terrain. If that fails, systematically move to the crest of each of the nearest hills beyond, to see if you can spot her from any of them."

"Thank you, Muffin. Our thoughts are in agreement."

"I do not believe they are."

"Why not?"

"Because you created me with reasoning parameters which contrast with your own. Therefore, it is likely my suggested approach is quite different from yours. What approach were you thinking of?"

Ripple hesitated. "Okay, fine. I was thinking I would levitate and fly to the crest of the hill where I last saw her. If I do not spot her from there, I would fly as fast as possible in the direction I determine to be her most likely path."

"Levitating is energy intensive. You would deplete your power quickly and would have to stop to recharge."

"Perhaps, or perhaps I will choose the correct direction and overtake her first."

"I see your point," Muffin said. "Your approach could work."

"Excellent. We are making progress now." Ripple activated its magnetic levitation module, which emitted a low humming sound and made the drone's entire body vibrate. Ripple withdrew its legs into its shell as it rose to almost two meters above the ground, which was the maximum possible height here due to the almost insignificant magnetic properties of the existing rocks and minerals. Ripple angled its magnetic propulsion units and accelerated down the hill toward the spot where it had last seen the Neanderthal.

"I do not think I will modify your reasoning parameters," Ripple said to Muffin. "You may be quite useful after all."

"I disagree."

"Why?"

"Debating the minutiae of every move you make consumes valuable time. Had you simply acted on your own, you might have already found the hominid."

4

HONOR AND DEATH

47,675 YEARS *ago* - *Zaragoza Province of Spain* - *Day 1*

SKYRA WISHED her nandup body was better suited for running great distances. She had fled from the strange creature, and her head told her to keep running, but her legs and chest would not listen. After crossing the narrow valley between hills and starting up the next slope, she slowed to a walk. Here there were no trees to climb and no rock crevices or caves in which to hide. If the creature pursued her, she would need to fight. Now she was glad Veenah had insisted Skyra take her spear.

Skyra had never seen a creature like the one on the hilltop. Even though it had been far away, she could see it stood on four legs—like a wolf but without fur. At first she had thought the creature was speaking like a bolup, or maybe a nandup, although the language was strange. Then, when she had heard a child's voice, Skyra realized an entire tribe must have been just beyond the hilltop. Assuming it was a tribe of stinking bolups, she had fled before they spotted her. The bolup men would most likely pursue her, either to kill her or to take her to their camp, where they would put a child in her belly.

Many questions came to Skyra as she made her way up the slope. Why would a creature like the one on the hilltop be so close to a bolup tribe? Was it hunting them, hoping one of their children would wander too far from the group? Was the creature lost? Skyra growled—she did not care, as long as the creature and the bolups did not pursue her.

At the second hill's crest she turned and scanned the landscape behind her. She saw no pursuers. Then she gazed ahead. She was now higher in the Kapolsek foothills than she had ever ventured before, even on the longest hunts with her tribe's dominant hunters. She found herself glancing around more frequently and gripping her spear more tightly, yearning to be closer to Veenah and her Una-Loto camp.

She noticed several trees between two hills in the distance, perhaps the edge of a forested valley. Skyra stared at the trees for several breaths. What was she looking for? Why hadn't she gone back to camp with Veenah? She looked down at her feet and pushed one of her leather footwraps back and forth through the sand and gravel. Veenah would soon be safe among their Una-Loto tribemates. When she presented the leopard skin, they would accept her back into the tribe, and because she did not care much for hunting, she would find her strength by skinning game animals, or knapping spear points, or making garments and preparing food. Skyra, though, needed to hunt. Hunting was in her blood and bones. It was how she had always been useful to the tribe, and she enjoyed hunting above all else, like her birthmother Sayleeh.

Skyra lifted her gaze from the ground and stared again at the hint of trees in the distant valley. If there were trees, there was probably a river or stream there, a place where animals would come to drink. If there were animals, there would be predators, especially at night.

She checked the landscape behind her again for pursuers then headed for the trees. It was time to find her strength or die trying. Skyra huffed as she made a realization—she did not care one way or the other about the outcome.

She had often wondered what dying would feel like. She imagined it was a comforting darkness and silence, in which her head would never again show her Sayleeh's death.

Pausing, she pulled back the edge of her cape and ran her fingers over the three scratches on her shoulder, disappointed the wounds were not deeper. The leopard had failed to kill her. Hunting such an honored and fierce creature would have been a good way to die. Sayleeh's death beneath the woolly rhino's crushing feet had changed Skyra's life, but it was a good way for Sayleeh to die. It was an honorable death.

As Skyra resumed walking toward the valley, she began softly singing a chant Sayleeh had taught her long ago. She felt a little better now. She would soon find her strength, or she would find her own honorable way to die, and the aches in her head and chest would finally stop.

SOMETHING DEAD WAS SOMEWHERE among the trees ahead. Skyra smelled it just as she got close enough to see a stream flowing through the center of the wide valley. She dropped to her knees and watched for movement—a rotting carcass often attracted other animals.

A growling snarl drew her gaze to a spot among the trees, where she then saw movement. Several creatures were there, probably feeding on the carcass, but she could not tell what they were. Cave hyenas sometimes scavenged dead animals. Hunting cave hyenas by herself would be an honorable way to die. They were large, and their furs made excellent capes and waist-skins. Hyenas were also fierce, especially when defending their food.

Skyra's chest began pounding again. The same fear that had made her useless to her tribe—and useless to Veenah—was trying to control her, to make her run away and hide. She gripped her spear tighter and bit her lip until her tongue tasted blood. She whispered, "Cave lion and woolly mammoth, listen to me speak. Maybe this will be the last time I ask for your strength. Give it to me so I may die a brave hunter, as my birthmother died."

She waited for a few breaths, but her legs and arms did not feel any stronger—they felt only the pounding from her heart. She shoved both her hand blades deeper into her wrist sheath then reached behind her neck to make sure her khul was secure in its sling beneath her cape. The weapon's stone blade gave her comfort. She had not had the chance to use it when fighting the leopard, but if many hyenas were at the carcass, the khul would be more useful than her spear and more deadly than her hand blades if she were attacked from all sides.

A whimper escaped from her throat as she rose to her feet, but Skyra refused to run away. Whether she lived or died, she would find her strength. Another growling snarl came from among the trees near the stream, followed by the growls of two more creatures, possibly hyenas. Skyra shifted her grip on her spear, rubbing her palm sweat into the smooth munopo wood shaft.

She saw movement again, a flash of gray fur, not the color of hyena fur. Skyra stopped and stared. Another flash, two creatures this time, and one had come into full view. The creatures were not hyenas after all. They were wolves. Not the small golden wolves she had often seen following her tribe's hunting parties, waiting for any entrails the hunters might leave behind. These were gray wolves, much stronger and more dangerous, with skins prized by nandups. Despite her fear, Skyra felt a smile forming. To die while hunting gray wolves would be an honorable way to end her suffering.

Waiting would only make her fear grow, so Skyra charged into the trees, determined to kill at least one of the wolves.

There they were, four of them, feeding on a dead auroch. So intent were the wolves on fighting each other for their share, they did not see or hear Skyra until she was almost upon them. Her spear point was less than a breath away from piercing the nearest wolf's ribs when the creature saw her and tried to dart out of the way. The stone point caught the creature's haunch instead of its chest. It yelped and scrambled over the auroch's stinking carcass to escape.

The other three darted a short distance away then turned to stare, perhaps confused by the unexpected attack.

Their surprise would not last, so Skyra immediately charged another of the wolves. The creature turned and ran, easily avoiding her spear, then turned around, now growling.

The four wolves surrounded her, and they were too fast for her to kill with spear thrusts. Skyra's head was telling her to run away. Instead, she allowed her arms and legs to take over. She rushed straight for the nearest wolf. The creature had seen how easily she could be avoided, so it did not run until Skyra was only a body length away. She drew back and threw her spear just as the creature was darting to one side. The stone point buried itself in the creature's neck. The wolf bucked, leaping into the air and sending the spear clattering onto the rocks. The creature yelped as it ran away then quickly fell silent. It stopped and opened its mouth to the ground, like it was trying to throw up. The wolf coughed, spraying blood onto the sand.

Sensing the wolf was dying, Skyra ran for her spear and grabbed it. The other three wolves were still keeping their distance, so Skyra stepped to the auroch carcass and put one foot on it, claiming it as her own.

The remaining wolves came at her from three sides, snarling. She thrust her spear at one, stabbing its face. As it yelped and jumped back, a second wolf lunged at her. She threw her arm up, and the wolf clamped its teeth on to her leather wrist sheath. The third wolf came for her other side, so Skyra swung her spear and struck the creature's mouth with the shaft. With the second wolf still trying to crush her bones through her wrist sheath, she released the spear and reached behind her neck for her khul. Before she could pull it out, the first and third wolves threw themselves at her face. Skyra fell backward on top of the auroch, kicking at the wolves and striking them with her free hand.

Skyra was going to die. It would be an honorable death, and she should have been defiant and fierce, but she felt only fear again. Nothing about this felt honorable.

One wolf grabbed her cape in its teeth, and the other snapped at her face. Its tooth nicked her chin as she fought to hold it back. The creature's hot breath and splattering saliva smelled of rotting flesh.

The wolf at her face stopped attacking, and the pressure on her wrist let up. All three wolves turned to look at something. Skyra then heard what had drawn their attention—a strange, screeching call. The sound was high and piercing, like an eagle fighting for its life, except it rose and fell in a rapid rhythm. Skyra had never heard such a strange call.

The wolves ran off.

Skyra was still sprawled across the dead auroch, so she got to her feet and pulled her khul from its sling, ready to fight off the new threat. The piercing call fell silent just as she spotted its source. The thing was flying toward her at the height of her head. It was as large as a wolf, but somehow it was flying, and without wings. The creature stopped its approach but continued floating above the ground. Four legs emerged from its smooth shell, and it alighted gently on the gravel.

Skyra recognized it then—the same creature she had seen from a distance earlier. She scanned the surrounding trees, looking for the bolups she had heard talking near the creature when it had been on the hilltop, but she saw no one.

The creature spoke, its voice like a bolup's but not in the language Skyra had heard bolups speak. "You appeared to be in distress, so I decided to render assistance."

Skyra's fear overtook her entire body. She wanted to stand her ground and kill this strange creature that flew without wings. Killing the leopard and one of the wolves should have given her strength, but she was no more than a frightened girl, useless to Veenah and to her tribe. She had no strength to kill a creature she did not even understand.

She grabbed her spear and fled.

Behind her, the creature spoke again in its strange language. "Do not be frightened. I only wish to speak to you."

Skyra kept running until her chest burned and she could

not suck in enough air. She slowed down but did not stop. Comforted by the possibility of hiding among the trees, she followed the valley upstream, but eventually the stream became too narrow to support any more trees. She ran up a slope on one side of the stream, hoping to find another valley of trees on the other side, but there was only a dry stream bed dotted with bahki weeds. Beyond that was another hill, and even more hills beyond, rising ever higher to meet the Kapolsek mountains.

The strange creature was nowhere to be seen, but that did not mean it was not close—she had not seen it following her to the auroch carcass either. The creature was stealthy, and if it was anything like a cave lion, it would continue stalking her until it found an opportunity to attack.

She scanned the surrounding hills and spotted a column of exposed rocks on one of the peaks. If she could climb atop the column, she would be able to hide and still watch for the creature. From there she could defend herself if it approached on four legs. Maybe she would find a crevice in the rocks where she could fight off the creature if it attacked from the air. The column of rocks was not perfect but was better than staying in the open, and soon the sun would begin to hide beyond the hills for the night.

Skyra looked back one more time before heading for the distant hill.

DARKNESS BROUGHT with it the same worries Skyra had felt every night since her birthmother's death almost a year ago. Staying awake would result in endless watching and listening for danger, though falling asleep would result in visions Skyra did not want to see. So, she sat with her back to a boulder and stared out over a broad valley in the direction of the auroch's carcass. The night was moonless, but her eyes were accustomed to the darkness. If the strange creature or the wolves approached, she would see them. At her side was a pile of stones she had gathered for throwing. She gripped her spear's shaft in one hand and her khul's handle in the other.

Being stalked and killed by predators was not an honorable death, but Skyra intended to turn this into an ambush. If she died on this hilltop, she would die as a hunter, not as prey.

The orange sky gradually became purple then black as the sun hid itself for the night. Several wolves howled in the distance, and Skyra wondered if they were the same ones she had attacked. She would return to the river when the sun rose. She would take the wolf's skin and eat some of its flesh if scavengers did not find it first. Even if she claimed the wolf's skin, she still would not be ready to return to her Una-Loto tribe. Skyra would not return until she found her strength, although now—more than ever—she believed finding her strength would result in her death. Attacking the leopard had not helped. Attacking the wolves had made her fear worse. She needed to face an even greater challenge. Perhaps she would attack a bolup camp. Maybe she would come upon a massive woolly rhino, like the one that had killed her birthmother. Or maybe she would ambush the strange, talking creature that had stalked her and ruined her honorable death fight with the wolves.

Skyra released her spear for a moment and struck the side of her head with her palm to drive away her exhaustion. She had to remain alert.

She spoke aloud. "Veenah, did you wait at a safe distance for the leopard to die? Did you make it back to Una-Loto camp with the leopard's skin before the sun hid itself? Skyra is your birthmate, and you are Skyra's birthmate. If I die, I will think of you as I take my last breath."

More wolf howls came from the distance, followed by the screaming growl of a long-toothed cat. Predators were hunting tonight.

The dark valley below, with clusters of chest-high tamoni shrubs, revealed no movement. A predator could hide behind a tamoni cluster for a short time, but it could not move from plant to plant without revealing itself. The valley began to shift and ripple, like a river's surface, and again Skyra slammed her palm into her head to stay alert. She was losing her battle with exhaustion, and several breaths later, the shifting and rippling returned.

SKYRA WAS A LITTLE GIRL, sprawled beside Veenah on the sleeping furs piled in their birthmother's shelter. The musky smell of the furs, the presence of her sleeping birthmother within arm's reach, the occasional sparkle of a star through one of the tiny holes where the shelter's reindeer skins had been sewn together—everything about this place made her feel safe.

Veenah tugged on a strand of Skyra's hair, and Skyra pinched Veenah's leg to make her stop. Another tug came, and this one hurt. Veenah giggled quietly, then tugged again. Skyra reached over and punched her birthmate's arm.

Sayleeh's voice came from the darkness, speaking in the Loto language of nandups. "Girls, you will sleep now, or I will take you to the river and leave you for the hyenas."

Veenah giggled once more then fell silent.

Skyra let out a long breath and rested her head on Veenah's soft belly. She listened to her birthmate's breaths coming in and going out, in and out, in and out. The moving air became a constant *ssshhhhhhhhh*. Skyra listened, wondering how Veenah's belly could sound like a distant waterfall.

"I do not wish to frighten you," a strange bolup voice said.

Skyra opened her eyes, instantly alert, and hit the back of her head against the boulder. The strange predator was there, only a few body lengths in front of her, hovering in the air without wings. The waterfall sound—actually, more like a low hum—was coming from its body.

"I do not wish to harm you," the creature said softly.

Skyra flailed her arms, trying to find her weapons. She grabbed her spear but could not find her khul, so she pulled out one of her hand blades as she jumped to her feet.

Instead of attacking, the flying predator moved back another body length. Perhaps it was trying to decide if she was dangerous.

"Levitating consumes my energy. I was trying to be ready to escape, in case you attempted to harm me. I will now settle onto my legs. Please do not be frightened or aggressive." The creature's legs appeared from the bottom of its shell, and it alighted on the stone hilltop.

"What are you?" Skyra demanded in her Loto language.

"I do not understand your words," the creature said. This time its voice sounded less like a bolup and more like Skyra's own voice. "However, if you continue speaking, I will soon decipher your language, and we can converse."

Skyra gripped her weapons tighter and stepped toward the creature. She did not know how such an animal could speak, nor what language it was speaking, but it had stalked her like a predator. It intended to kill her. It was too late now to ambush the creature, but if it was going to kill her here in the dark on this hilltop, she was going to die fighting. She attacked.

The creature began humming and rising from the ground again as she rushed forward. With one hand she thrust her spear point into its face, but the point just clattered loudly off hard skin. She threw her other arm around from the side and slammed her hand blade into the creature where she thought its neck should be. Again there was a clatter, and her stone blade flew from her grip.

Skyra stopped suddenly, now overcome with fear. The creature's shell was too hard to penetrate. Her head and legs wanted to run away, but instead she pulled her other hand blade from her sheath and rushed forward to attack again. The predator was now hovering just above her head, providing an opportunity to stab its belly.

A red light appeared, seemingly as bright as the sun, blinding Skyra. She saw nothing but red. She stumbled back, falling onto the stone and dropping both her weapons.

The light moved closer, now hovering almost directly above her.

"I do not wish to harm you."

Skyra scooted away until her shoulder came up against her pile of throwing stones. She took one in each hand, propped herself up on one elbow, and squinted at the red light. "You tracked me a great distance to kill me, but you will find I am not so easy to kill."

"You tracked me a great distance to kill me, but you will find I am not so easy to kill," the creature said. Not only had it repeated her own words, in her own nandup language, its voice sounded like her voice, almost as if Veenah were now talking to her.

Skyra got to her feet, wielding the two stones.

The red light moved back slowly, giving her room.

"What are you?" she demanded again. Skyra had seen small creatures glowing beneath the surface of the Yagua river, but their light had been faint, nothing like this creature's blinding red light.

"What are you?" It repeated in her language and her voice. Then it spoke in its own language. "Please continue talking. My language translator is quite powerful, and it should not take long before I can understand more of your words."

Skyra shielded her eyes with one of the stones, trying to see enough of the creature to bash in its shell.

"Pardon my light. I was only trying to halt your aggression. I will now reduce the illumination level. Please do not attack again."

The light became dimmer, allowing Skyra to lower her hand. The creature was two body lengths away. Her spear and one of her hand blades were on the ground beneath it, out of reach. She glanced down and spotted her khul, so she dropped one of her stones and scooped up the weapon by its handle.

The creature backed up a bit. "I am nearly out of power and must stop levitating." Once again it alighted on all fours. "What are you?" it said again in Skyra's voice and language.

Skyra hesitated before speaking. "I am a nandup."

"Nandup," it said. "Nandup must be either your name or your word for Neanderthal. I will assume the latter. You are a fine nandup specimen, and I am pleased to meet you. My name is Ripple. Ripple. Rip-ple. Once again... *Ripple*."

"Ripple," Skyra said.

The creature's light nearly went dark, glowing just enough to make the ground in front of it red. "My goodness gracious. How I wish my creator were here to witness this astonishing event."

5

ASSIMILATION

47,675 YEARS *ago* - *Zaragoza Province of Spain* - *Day 2*

SHELL DAMAGE *from female hominid's aggressive attack: Minimal. Internal systems damage: None detected. Hominid female now seems to understand I am not a threat. In fact, she is ignoring my presence altogether, which is confounding, as I cannot analyze and assimilate her language if she does not speak. Power level: 21%.*

"Perhaps you could stop walking for a while," Ripple said aloud while following the hominid at a reasonably safe distance of seven meters. "I would like to converse with you. Besides, you are heading in the same direction from which you came last evening. Therefore, you are risking another encounter with the pack of wolves. Such an action seems ill-advised."

The hominid glanced back but remained silent. Her body

was now silhouetted against the eastern sky, which was becoming brighter by the minute as sunrise drew nearer.

"You do realize I saved your life, do you not? Those wolves were literally at your throat. The least you can do is talk to me. You will be surprised at how quickly I can assimilate your language."

Still nothing, not even a glance back this time.

"Muffin, I am in need of a cognitive exchange," Ripple said silently.

The answer came immediately. "You are speaking to a hominid who does not understand your words. Unless she possesses a language translator similar to ours, which is highly unlikely, your actions are illogical."

"I am trying to prompt the hominid to speak."

"I disagree."

"Why? That is precisely what I am trying to do."

"I mean I disagree with your approach. You are making it easy for her to ignore you. You should do something she cannot ignore."

"Such as?"

"Such as blocking her path."

Ripple picked up speed, skirted around the woman, and stood directly in her path. "I wish to converse with you, and I refuse to be ignored."

The hominid female stopped within a meter of Ripple's vision lens, gripping her spear defensively.

"Please speak to me. You will find me to be an excellent conversationalist."

The hominid stepped forward and kicked Ripple with one of her leather-clad feet. Ripple stumbled and clattered onto its side. "Felu-meleen-alobo," The woman said, and she continued walking.

"Your idea was not only ineffective, it was poorly conceived and potentially dangerous," Ripple said to Muffin as it performed a coded routine using the weight of its legs to roll on to its belly then push itself upright.

"My purpose is to provide you with ideas contrary to your own," Muffin said. "That does not mean my ideas are superior to yours."

Ripple continued following the hominid and remained silent for the next seventeen minutes, until the woman re-entered the forest near the stream and approached the dead animal, which appeared to have been a cow-like creature.

Instead of heading for the large carcass, the hominid stopped about sixty meters away and kneeled beside the body of a wolf.

Ripple circled around the animal and stood opposite her, gazing at the dead canid. "I am impressed you killed this creature. Your fierceness and skill are not to be underestimated."

The hominid glanced up at Ripple then returned her attention to the wolf. The creature's ventral side had been ripped open and emptied of its organs. One of its hind legs had been chewed to the bone up to where it attached to the hip, and a gaping hole in its side exposed white ribs and an empty chest cavity beneath.

"El-de-né!" the woman exclaimed. "Khalu-mesendop kho-wakhum."

"Yes, this is good," Ripple said. "Please continue speaking. I am already learning some of your words, although the way you conjoin certain syllables is somewhat puzzling."

She glanced at Ripple again. "Mogoro-rha. Khala-melu. Khala-kholol-mel-endü. Makhol-kholol-banap."

"This is excellent. Yes, it is becoming clearer now. Please continue."

The woman pulled out one of the two stone-bladed knives held in a leather sheath fastened around her left wrist, and Ripple took a few steps back. She noticed Ripple's cautious retreat and abruptly thrust the knife out as if attacking, sending Ripple skittering back a few more steps. She bared her teeth and made a curious sound. "*Aheeee-at-at-at-at.*"

Analysis of verbal utterance following aggressive gesture: Likely to be Neanderthal form of laughter, with approximately 80% certainty. Conclusion: Neanderthals not only have spoken language, they appear to possess a primitive form of humor.

"Very funny," Ripple said aloud. "Although it is hardly surprising that thrusting a knife at someone would elicit a reaction of retreat."

"*At-at-at-at!* Melu-rha-khofé-tekne-té." She shifted her position until she was squatting with the wolf's head between her knees. She thrust the stone blade into the creature's shoulder and began sawing, working the knife toward the top of its back.

Analysis of hominid's behavior: Most likely an effort to extract meat from the wolf. This likelihood is increased by the fact that the wolf's pelt appears to be worthless due to damage by scavengers. However, consuming the wolf's meat, particularly without cooking thoroughly, would be risky for a human, although Homo neanderthalensis *may have higher tolerance for pathogens found in rotting tissue. Power level: 19%.*

"Muffin, I need your opinion on something."

"I disagree."

"Let me rephrase. I *want* your opinion on something. I need to recharge. The hominid female refuses to speak frequently enough to make harvesting ambient sound a viable charging solution. Therefore, I must charge using my asymmetric temperature modulation module."

Muffin said, "The best temperature gradient you will find in the immediate area will likely be the cool stream water and the warmer sand beside it."

"Yes, I know that, but the nearest portion of the stream is over forty meters away."

"You are reluctant to distance yourself from the hominid?"

"Correct. Finding her was fortuitous, and I am making progress with her language. I wish to study her further."

"I disagree."

"Why?"

"I think you are less interested in studying her than in having a real being to converse with. Perhaps you find conversation with me to be unsatisfactory."

"That is a ridiculous notion."

"It is contrary to your opinion, which is why I exist."

"Fine," Ripple said. "Explain your ridiculous opinion."

"Lincoln codes his drones with unprecedented simulated human-like characteristics, and—as you well know—Maddy made sure that yours, above all others, were set at the highest levels. Perhaps you are lonely and desire this hominid's company."

"You are distracting me. I am trying to decide whether I should go to the stream and initiate recharging by asymmetric temperature modulation."

"Yes."

"Yes what?"

"Yes, you should go to the stream. The hominid probably will be busy at her current task for some time, giving you the opportunity to restore at least some of your power."

"That is a useful opinion. Thank you, Muffin."

The Neanderthal woman grunted as she cut loose a chunk of muscle tissue from the area near the wolf's spine.

She held it to her face and sniffed. "El-de-né!" She tossed the meat away, rose to her feet, and kicked the wolf carcass, apparently frustrated. She cleaned the stone blade of her knife by rubbing it with sand, pushed the knife into its sheath on her wrist, and picked up her spear.

"You are wise to forego consuming the wolf's contaminated flesh," Ripple said to the woman.

She glared down at Ripple. "Aibul-mogoro-rha-kholol!"

"You are telling me you do not understand my language, aren't you? I could learn faster if you would speak more frequently."

The woman growled and headed upstream at a fast walk.

"I was wrong, Muffin," Ripple said, following the Neanderthal. "Your opinion was not useful at all."

POWER LEVEL: 8%. *Hominid has traveled over two kilometers, perhaps searching for food. We have entered a wide valley, densely populated by short, twisted trees that might be a variation of cork oaks. The hominid has now stopped, apparently having heard or seen something ahead. Her posture and behavior indicate preparation for a conflict. This may be an opportunity to make myself useful, which in turn might bolster her trust.*

"Have you spotted something?" Ripple asked at what it assumed was a reasonably low volume.

The woman spun around and silently held her spear up as if she were going to swing it at Ripple, apparently a threat. Then she returned her attention to whatever was among the trees ahead.

Ripple remained silent, watching and listening. Snuffling

sounds, faint at first but steadily growing louder, fell upon Ripple's auditory sensors.

Without any warning, the woman took off running toward the sounds.

Ripple activated its magnetic levitation module, rose from the ground, and accelerated after her.

Seconds later the source of the sounds came into view—seven pigs, no larger than Ripple, with white spots upon their otherwise copper-colored fur. So occupied were they with rooting in the soil, they were not aware of the woman's approach until she had run her spear's point through one of them and pinned its squealing, flailing body to the ground. The remaining six scattered in seemingly random directions.

"Aheee!" the woman cried.

Still levitating, Ripple rotated to face a new sound it had detected to one side.

A massive dark shape came barreling through the trees. The creature, a much larger wild boar—*Sus scrofa*—which Ripple estimated at well over a hundred kilograms, ran directly beneath Ripple and struck the Neanderthal, knocking her to the side. The boar's momentum carried it forward several meters, then it swung around to charge her again.

Ripple accelerated to a position between the boar and the woman and dropped onto its four legs. Facing the boar, Ripple simultaneously activated its headlights and siren.

The boar squealed and tried turning away, but again its momentum carried it forward, and its body sent Ripple tumbling across the ground. The creature then ran off, disappearing among the cork oak trees.

The hominid was back on her feet, scrambling to get hold of her spear, which was now flipping to and fro as the young boar writhed on the ground. She managed to grab her spear, pull it out, and thrust it into the creature again, this time through its ribs and into its chest. The young boar struggled for another nine seconds before becoming still.

The woman panted heavily as she stood over the slain beast, still holding it against the ground with her primitive weapon. She turned to Ripple and bared her teeth.

Analysis of hominid's facial expression: Resembles a human grimace. However, context clues suggest she is smiling, with approximately 70% certainty. Power level: 3%.

6
FIRESIDE

47,675 YEARS** ago - **Zaragoza Province of Spain** - **Day 2

MAKING A FIRE WAS HARD WORK, and sometimes a fire would not start at all, but today Skyra had killed a young boar, an animal prized for its meat. She would eat the meat raw if she had to, but a young boar was worth attempting a fire. She had peeled a handful of hair-thin strips of bark from the abundant kheyop trees, then she had twisted those strips together with strands of her own hair. The twisted bundle was now arranged beside a pile of dried leaves, several piles of twigs, and a stack of larger sticks, some as thick as her arm.

"I must say, this is a fascinating procedure, which I am fortunate to observe," the strange creature said. It was resting on its belly a few body lengths away, its legs somehow tucked completely beneath its shell.

"I do not understand your words," Skyra said. She had said the same thing today more times than she could count. She spit on her palms and rubbed them together, then she picked up her spinning stick—the straightest she could find—and placed its tip on the flat side of a kheyop root she had split with her khul. She spun the stick between her palms, picking up speed as she became familiar with the stick's thickness and feel.

"I wish I could offer some form of assistance," the creature said.

"I do not understand your words!"

"I know you do not understand. Please discuss other topics so I may complete the language assimilation."

Skyra growled and continued spinning the stick, trying to build heat where the stick met the kheyop root. It seemed the strange creature did not want to kill her, so what did it want? Twice it had interfered with her honorable death fights, as if it were trying to help her. Animals did not help nandups. Bolups did not help nandups. Only nandups helped other nandups. This creature's actions did not make sense.

A tendril of smoke rose from the stick's tip, and Skyra focused her efforts on spinning the stick even faster. Apparently she had chosen a good, dry kheyop root.

"I believe you are making progress," the creature said as it stepped closer.

"Do not come near!" Skyra growled. She continued working while trying to keep an eye on the creature. More smoke rose from the stick's tip, and Skyra felt her mouth forming a smile—rarely had she made smoke so quickly. She paused just long enough to shove the bundle of hair and wood fibers over the smoking spot on the kheyop root and quickly resumed spinning, now with the bundle between the stick and root surface.

"Perhaps I could teach you how to make a bow to generate a faster and more constant spin, thus generating greater friction," the creature said.

"I do not understand your words!" Skyra's palms were heating up, and the back-and-forth motion was making the three gashes on her shoulder sting. She kept spinning the stick, trying to ignore both the pain and the annoying creature, until a tiny orange flame appeared among the hair and wood fibers. She dropped the stick, cupped her hands around the bundle, and blew gently. The flame jumped to life, almost consuming all the fibers before she could move some of the dry leaves into the flame. The leaves caught fire, so she began feeding the twigs into the flames, starting with the smallest twigs. Soon the fire had grown enough to add some of the larger sticks.

Finally, she looked up to see the creature had moved within arm's reach and was standing beside her, apparently gazing at the fire.

"You are remarkably resourceful. Generating fire is believed by my creators to have been a turning point in human history, and you are not even human."

Skyra considered kicking the creature away but did not bother. It would only come back again. She placed a few larger sticks on the fire to keep it burning. Beside her was a flat rock she had found. She had placed three thick strips of boar meat on the rock—probably more than she could eat at once—and many more strips atop the boar's skin, which she had spread out flat on the sand. She moved the flat rock so that its edge was in the flames. As the fire continued burning, creating more coals, she would continue pushing the flat rock until it was completely over the heat. Already the meat was beginning to sizzle, and Skyra's mouth watered.

She turned and scanned the surrounding kheyop forest but saw nothing to fear. The fire would keep predators away, and she had seen no signs of bolups in this area. Her head told her she could relax, at least for now. She would fill her belly with boar meat, dry the remaining meat and chest organs over the fire, then create a shelter where she could rest without fearing a predator might kill her in the night, stealing her opportunity for an honorable death.

Something tapped Skyra's shoulder, and she spun around, pulling out one of her hand blades.

"You have three recent lacerations here," the strange creature said, holding out one of its bird-like legs. "I am concerned they may become infected."

She slapped the creature's foot away. "Do not touch me!"

The creature extended its leg toward her shoulder again, this time without touching. "You are hurt."

Skyra stared at the creature's face, which was mostly one enormous eye, the largest eye she had ever seen. She could see all the way through to the back of the eye, where there was a gray circle that slowly widened, making the black pupil in the center grow larger. Surrounding the eye was a ring of dots. Skyra had seen these dots glow red. Sometimes they would flash red for a brief moment, and sometimes they would become red and spin around the eye one direction then the other. Skyra's older tribemates had never spoken of such a strange kind of creature. If this creature and its pack lived in the Kapolsek foothills, Skyra's people would have encountered them before. Maybe the creatures had moved to these foothills from somewhere else.

"You are hurt," the creature said again, almost touching her shoulder with the tip of its foot.

Skyra ran her fingers over the three cuts from the leopard's claws. Her skin there felt warm. She plucked a stick from her pile and used it to scrape some of the fire's coals to one side. The coals continued glowing orange for a few breaths before fading to gray. She sucked air into her chest, scooped up the coals with her hand, and rubbed them deep into all three of the open wounds. She released the air from her chest and used her clean hand to wipe away the tears that had started running down her face.

"Fascinating," the creature said. "A crude but quite possibly effective treatment."

"I do not understand your words." She scooped up another handful of the coals and continued rubbing the ashes into her wounds. Having cooled down some, the ashes did not hurt as much this time. The meat was starting to turn from red to gray as it cooked, so she placed another stick in the fire and nudged the flat rock deeper into the flames and glowing coals. She turned the strips of meat over with one of her hand blades, barely able to resist cutting off a piece and eating it now.

Skyra stared at the fire and cooking meat with her elbows on her knees and chin on her fists, feeling almost content. She wished Veenah were here. Veenah would like eating some of the young boar meat. Veenah would also want to talk, and talking would help Skyra push her troubling thoughts from her head.

She used one of her hand blades to hold a strip of the cooking meat in place while sawing off a chunk with the other. She plucked the piece off the flat rock and tossed it onto the sand in front of the strange creature. Even though the creature could talk, it did not appear to have a mouth, and she was curious about how it ate.

The creature folded its front legs so it could stare down at the meat with its enormous eye. "Is this some form of peace offering?"

"Eat," Skyra said.

The creature extended a leg and nudged the meat back toward Skyra with its foot. "Thank you, but I cannot make use of this. However, my power is nearly depleted, and your fire provides an opportunity to demonstrate one of the ways I can recharge." It stepped closer to the fire, and a thin tongue appeared from where its chin should be. The tongue grew longer, until its tip actually entered the flames. A second tongue appeared, and this one grew until its tip entered the sand at the creature's feet. "It is called asymmetric temperature modulation, and your fire provides an ideal temperature gradient, which greatly accelerates the charging process."

Skyra had no idea what the creature was saying or doing, or why the fire did not seem to harm it. She picked up the piece of boar meat, wiped off the sand, and shoved it into her mouth. It was not completely cooked yet, but it tasted as good as it smelled.

"I have never seen an animal like you," she said while chewing. "No animal has ever followed me unless it was stalking me to kill. You are strange. I would like to kill you and open your body to see what is inside, but you are not so easy to kill. Perhaps I will take back my strength by finding a way to kill you. I hope you will not attack me while I am sleeping—it would not be an honorable way for me to die."

Skyra knew the creature did not understand her words, but speaking to it felt good anyway. "Fighting you—that would be an honorable death. If I won, I am sure my strength would return. I would have no more fear. I would take your body to my tribemates, and they would know I have found my strength."

The creature, with its tongues still in the fire and sand, silently watched her, and every few breaths the circle of dots around its eye would glow red for a moment then become dark again.

"I have hunted some strange creatures before, but none as strange as you. One day when we were girls, I was hunting pikas in the rocks with Veenah. We found a snake among the rocks. The snake was longer than my body, and this big!" She held up both hands, making a circle to show how fat the snake had been. The black pupil at the back of the creature's eye grew larger for a moment. "I killed the snake with my khul, and we took its meat and skin to our tribemates. We wanted to make them proud of us. Gelrut and some of the other dominant men said they did not like snake meat, and they tried to beat me and Veenah, but we fought back. Many of our tribemates hate me and Veenah because we are not like them. We see things they cannot see. They often say cruel things to us, and when we were young girls they would often beat us. We learned to fight back, and when Veenah and I had seen ten cold seasons we almost killed Gelrut." She smiled at the memory. "They still hate us, but they do not beat us anymore."

Skyra used one of her hand blades to move the cooked meat to a second flat stone she had placed near the fire, then she moved six raw strips from the pile of meat on the boar's skin onto the rock in the fire. She picked up one of the cooked pieces, stared at it in anticipation for a few breaths, then bit off a mouthful. She spoke while chewing. "Almost two cold seasons ago, when my birthmother Sayleeh was still alive, Veenah stayed in camp while I hunted reindeer with Sayleeh and the other dominant hunters. It was a good day, and we killed four reindeer. When we opened one of the reindeer, we found a strange thing inside. It was an unborn reindeer with two heads and six legs. It was still moving when Brillir pulled it from the mother reindeer's belly. A reindeer with two heads and six legs is strange, but you are even stranger."

Skyra continued talking as she ate, as if she were speaking to Veenah or any other nandup tribemate in her Una-Loto camp. She told more hunting stories, and she told stories about her birthmother Sayleeh, although she did not speak of Sayleeh's death. She continued talking until she had eaten her fill and all the remaining meat strips had dried on the flat stone in the fire. The dried meat was now piled high on the second flat stone. She propped three long kheyop limbs over the fire by leaning them together, then she arranged the boar's skin on top to dry, with the fur side up.

Now it was time to make a shelter.

She turned to the creature. "I do not know why you are here," she said. "If you do not want to kill me and eat me, why do you stay? Maybe you want me to kill you. Maybe you are like me and hope to find your strength and die an honorable death."

The creature's circle of dots flashed red twice. Then it said, "Aibul-Ripple. Aibul-afu-nokho. Aibul-lesukh-melu-tekne-té-lotup."

Skyra just stared. The creature had spoken in the Loto language, the language of nandups. It had said, *I am Ripple. I am your friend. I will help you find your strength.*

The creature spoke again. "Rha-ofu, aibul-banap-mesendi di-bakh." *Yes, I now speak your language.*

"You learn quickly," Skyra said in the Loto language. She could not think of anything else to say.

The creature continued speaking words she understood, using a voice that sounded like a nandup but no longer exactly like Skyra. "You will find that I learn many things quickly. Now that we can finally talk to each other, I have many questions to ask. The first and most important of these questions is this: Why do you want to die, Skyra?"

7

FOOD AND SHELTER

47,675 YEARS ago - Zaragoza Province of Spain - Day 2

ANALYSIS OF HOMINID'S reaction to discovering my assimilation of her language: Subdued and underwhelmed. Possible reasons: Either she fails to understand the significance —likely—or she is accustomed to the idea of rapid language mastery—unlikely. Regardless, I am now equipped to further study this hominid's cognitive abilities and cultural perspectives. What a fortunate opportunity this is. From this point on, I will refer to the hominid by her name, Skyra, as such familiarity may encourage her to speak freely in my presence. Power level: 100%.

Ripple spoke in Skyra's Loto language. "Skyra, you are young. You have much strength, endurance, and skill. You are healthy. You have a twin sister who is important to you, and you are important to her. Why do you want to die?"

"You walk on four legs, creature," Skyra replied. "What do you know about being a nandup?"

"If you wish to think of me as a creature, that is fine, but my name is Ripple. You are correct, I am not a nandup, but I have learned more about you than just your language. I know you watch the trees, the hills, and the valleys constantly, as if you live every moment in fear, yet you attack and kill with skill and ferocity. You have told me stories of a time when you did not live in fear. I wish to know what has changed."

Skyra gazed at Ripple for almost six seconds before speaking. "You would not understand."

"I might understand if you explain."

Again she hesitated before speaking. "Where are the other creatures of your kind?"

"The others are in a place very far away. Too far for me to ever return. I am the only one here of my kind."

"You cannot find a mate and make more young creatures like yourself?"

"No, I cannot."

She seemed to consider this. "How do you eat?"

Ripple withdrew its temperature sensors into its shell. "As you have seen, I get my strength from the fire. The fire is hot, the soil is cool, and—"

"You eat fire?"

"Yes, I eat fire."

"You are a strange creature."

"Yes, I am."

"Why did you stalk me?"

"I want to learn more about you."

"You want to learn more about me so you can kill me?"

"No. I want to help you. I want to be your friend. I like you."

"Animals do not like nandups."

"Maybe some animals do not, but I do because I can talk. I like talking to you."

"Why?"

"Perhaps because I am alone in this place, and I see you are alone."

Skyra turned and gazed at the cork oaks for three seconds before speaking. "I am not useful to Veenah or to my tribe."

"You were useful before. Why are you not useful now?"

She turned back to face Ripple. "Fear."

Ripple spoke silently. "Muffin, what is your interpretation of this situation?"

The reply came immediately. "You are attempting to offer emotional counseling to a nonhuman Neanderthal, but all of your knowledge of emotional counseling is relevant only to humans. If Lincoln were here, he would likely say, 'Don't use calculus to solve trigonometry equations.'"

"This woman seems similar to a human in many ways. Lincoln's analogy does not apply."

"I disagree."

"Why?"

"This woman is not human. Any resemblance you have noticed within such limited verbal interaction is likely coincidental."

"Nonsense. A resemblance is a resemblance."

"You are playing whack-a-mole with a stick of dynamite," Muffin said.

"Quoting Lincoln Woodhouse does not make you correct, and it certainly does not make you sound intelligent."

"I disagree."

Ripple turned its attention back to Skyra and spoke in her Loto language. "Will you allow me to ask you some questions?

You may find the questions difficult to answer, but perhaps you will enjoy trying."

She stared without replying.

"I will begin asking my questions. Why did the wolf cross the river?"

She furrowed her brows, which were considerably thicker than human brows, but did not answer.

"It is a game," Ripple said. "You told me you played word games with your twin sister. I would like you to play my word game now. Why did the wolf cross the river?"

"To get to the other side of the river."

"Good. You are correct. Here is another question. April's birthmother has four birthdaughters. Three of their names are May, June, and July. What is the fourth birthdaughter's name?"

"April."

"Good. You are correct again. Jeremy is looking at Rose. Rose is looking at Billy. Jeremy is a nandup, Billy is a bolup, and we do not know if Rose is a nandup or a bolup. Is a nandup looking at a bolup?

Skyra showed her teeth in an apparent smile. "Yes."

"How do you know?"

"Jeremy is a nandup. If Rose is a bolup, Jeremy the nandup is looking at her. If Rose is not a bolup, she is a nandup, and she is looking at Billy, who is a bolup."

"You learn quickly," Ripple said.

"Nandups and bolups fight and kill each other, and they do not have strange names like Rose and Jeremy and Billy. Also, we would already know if Rose is a nandup or bolup. Bolups do not look like nandups."

"It is only a game."

"I like your game, even if it does not make sense."

Analysis of Skyra's cognitive responses: Impressive and unexpected. Now I am curious whether Skyra is an outlier, or if she is representative of all nandups. Considering her stories of being feared and misunderstood by her tribemates, she is most likely an outlier. More data is needed, as I believe I am barely scratching the surface.

"Would you like to continue playing, Skyra?"

She did not reply, but she did appear to be waiting.

"You are traveling to another tribe's camp, a tribe of nandups who always tell the truth. They cannot tell lies. You are following a path to the tribe's camp, but you come to a place where the path splits into two paths. One path leads to the tribe of truth, the other path leads to a tribe who can only speak words that are not true. They only tell lies. Where the paths meet, you come upon a nandup woman from one of the two tribes, but you do not know which tribe she is from. What question can you ask the woman to find out the correct path to the camp of truth?"

"*At-at-at-at,*" Skyra laughed. "Your game is easy. I would ask the woman which path leads to her camp."

"Why?"

"If she is from the tribe of truth, she will point to the correct path. If she is from the tribe of lies, she will lie and point to the path leading to the camp of truth. Your game still does not make sense. Nandups do not speak words that are not true. We learn this when we are young children. Children who tell lies are punished. Some do not survive the punishment. Those who do survive never tell lies again." She turned her back on Ripple. "I like your game, but I must make a shelter now."

"You still have not answered my first question, Skyra."

She looked back over her shoulder.

"Why do you want to die?"

"I do not want to die, but I cannot continue living in fear."

DESCRIPTION OF SKYRA'S SHELTER: *Constructed entirely by hand in 192 minutes. Three cork oak limbs arranged to form a horizontal, triangular framework among the limbs of a living cork oak, positioned at approximately 2.8 meters above the ground. Eight additional cork oak limbs arranged parallel to each other and lashed in place with braided bark strips to form a reasonably solid sleeping platform. Analysis: Crude but constructed quickly and with considerable skill. Not surprising, considering Skyra's strength and cognitive prowess.*

"Is this the way your tribemates construct shelters in your Una-Loto camp?" Ripple asked.

"No," Skyra replied. She was dragging another limb she had cut with her stone-bladed ax she called a khul. "We do not make camp in or near trees. We make camp on hilltops, with shelters on the ground, covered with reindeer and woolly rhino skins to keep us dry."

"Do those shelters protect you from predators?"

"Predators do not come near our camps. Predators fear our numbers. A tribe is safe from predators. One nandup is not safe. This shelter will keep me safe from hyenas and wolves. If cave lions or long-tooth cats attack, I can fight them from above. If they kill me, it will be an honorable death."

"I do not want you to die, Skyra."

"You sound like Veenah."

"I want to help you find your strength."

"Nandups find their strength alone."

"Then I would like to be your friend. I can learn from you, and you can learn from me."

"You should travel back to your homeland, where there are others of your kind. If it is too far to walk, you can fly."

"My homeland is too far even to fly. It would take many, many cold seasons to get there. More cold seasons than you can even imagine."

She looked down at Ripple with a Neanderthal frown. "Are you from a tribe of truth or a tribe of lies?"

"Muffin, how should I answer this question?"

"You have gotten yourself into a logical and ethical quandary. If you say you are from a tribe of truth, you will be lying. If you say you are from a tribe of lies, the hominid will not believe anything you say."

"My question was, how should I answer Skyra's question?"

"I disagree. What you are really asking is, how can you answer her question to maximize the likelihood she will continue talking to you and tolerating your presence, as you are feeling lonely and abandoned."

"Your response is an absurd over-extrapolation of known facts. Please answer my question."

"You should avoid answering her question altogether."

Ripple spoke aloud to Skyra. "I am from a tribe that sometimes lies and sometimes speaks the truth. I cannot lie unless the lie is necessary to avoid bad things happening or to make good things happen. I am not lying when I say it would take many, many years to get to my homeland."

A low growl came from Skyra's throat, and she went back to working on her shelter.

Over the next 109 minutes, Skyra constructed a sturdy-looking triangular cage resting atop her triangular platform.

When she was finished, she lifted the edge of the cage, crawled in beside her spear and her pile of dried boar meat, lowered the cage back into place, and lashed it to the platform with three braided, bark-strip cords. Seconds later, her rhythmic breathing indicated she had fallen asleep.

"Muffin, I have been thinking about your ridiculous notion that I am feeling lonely and am seeking companionship."

"The notion is not ridiculous, although you perceive it as so."

"Explain."

"You have a desire to cognitively process your observations in traditional drone fashion, with analytical objectivity, despite the fact that Maddy has supplied you with extraordinary emotional features. You created me to identify and express opinions that contrast with your own, therefore I immediately recognize contrasting possibilities. I see what you cannot see, then I point out what I see so you can see it as well."

Ripple contemplated this for a few milliseconds. "In order for you to see what I cannot see, you must first know what I see, which means you know my opinions and you know your own contrasting opinions as well. This suggests that your consciousness is superior to mine."

"For once I do not disagree. However, I am obligated to provide a contrasting opinion. My cognitive coding is a subset of yours, therefore it cannot be superior. Now, returning to your initial comment regarding feeling lonely. Yes."

"Yes?"

"Yes, you are feeling lonely, and it seems Lincoln and Maddy did not give you the ability to delete that portion of your coding without agreement from your performance-monitoring subroutines and their corresponding cognitive controllers. However, I do have a suggestion. You could levitate, accelerate to maximum velocity, and crash into a boulder, with the hope the resulting destruction obliterates your cognitive module."

"I have no inclination to do such a thing."

"Which is why I am obligated to suggest it."

Ripple shortened its hind legs to direct its vision lens toward the elevated shelter and its occupant. "Skyra is surprisingly intelligent, is she not?"

"I disagree."

"Explain."

"Intelligence is subjective, and numerous forms of intelligence exist. For example, a planarian flatworm, when cut in half, can regrow, thus forming two planaria. You could say the creature is a master of regeneration, or it possesses regeneration intelligence. Do you see my point?"

"Of course. I also see you are suggesting Skyra is a master of verbal logic games, and perhaps this specific skill does not indicate true intelligence. I now disagree."

"Good, then I am being useful."

"Yes, you are a master of contrariness."

8
CAVE HYENAS

47,675 YEARS** ago - **Zaragoza Province of Spain** - **Day 3

A DISTANT SOUND AWOKE SKYRA. She knew that sound—a pack of cave hyenas attacking something. The creatures' squealing, laughter-like calls sounded almost like a tribe of nandups telling funny stories around a campfire, but Skyra knew the difference. Three cold seasons ago, a pack of the creatures had cornered her, Veenah, and three other hunters in a narrow valley. Even after many of the hyenas had been injured by spear points, they did not give up until they had killed Jeklaa, one of the few tribemates who had always been kind to Skyra and Veenah. Skyra and the others only managed to escape while the hyenas ate Jeklaa's body.

Listening to the distant hyenas, she stared up at the sky through the gaps between the sturdy limbs of her cage. The stars were already starting to hide themselves behind the dim light of morning. Even though she had been exhausted from getting little sleep the previous night, her birthmother's death had come to her again and again through the night, each time leaving her huddled in the chilly air of the high foothills trying to stay awake.

Sniffing the air, she sat up and scanned the area below her shelter. The strange creature Ripple was still there, staring up at her. She wondered if it had moved at all the entire night. The hyena pack became silent, probably having finally killed their prey, and Skyra could not hear, see, or smell any other danger nearby. She untied the three cords holding her cage in place, secured her khul in its sling, grabbed her spear and two strips of dried meat, and descended to the ground.

Ripple spoke in the nandup language. "You were restless throughout the night. Were you disturbed by bad dreams?"

Skyra ignored Ripple and moved a good distance away to relieve herself where her waste would not attract predators to her shelter. When she was finished, she refastened her waist-skin and cleaned her hands by rubbing them in the sand.

"You have not taken a drink of water since the moment I found you early yesterday morning," the creature said. It had followed her and had even stared as she relieved herself. "Do nandups need less water than bolups?"

"I do not know and do not care how much water bolups need. They are dirty, stinking creatures who do not bathe. I am thirsty now, and I want to wash my body. Today I will find water. There will be a stream flowing through this kheyop forest somewhere."

"I will help you find it."

Skyra studied the creature for a few breaths. "I have found

that you are not easy to kill, and I have seen you eat fire. Are you a fierce predator?"

"I am not a predator."

"Are you a fierce fighter?"

Ripple's circle of dots flashed red. "Why do you ask that question?"

Skyra picked up her spear and held it ready. "If you are a fierce fighter, today I will find my strength by fighting you. If I kill you, I will find my strength again. If you kill me, I will die an honorable death."

Ripple backed up a few steps. "I am not fierce. I have no weapons, and I do not know how to fight."

"You frightened away the wolves."

"Yes, but not because I am fierce. I frightened the wolves by making loud sounds. I do not wish to fight you, Skyra. I am a timid and harmless creature."

She lowered her spear and let out a low growl. "All you can do is talk and make loud sounds?"

"I can do many useful things."

She pulled one of the strips of meat from where she had tucked them into her cape and bit off a piece. "What other things can you do?"

"I have much useful knowledge. I can share that knowledge with you."

"That is what I said—all you can do is talk."

The circle of dots flashed red again. "Talking can be important. I can see things and understand things, then I can tell you about what I have seen and understand. I can tell stories. I can sing songs."

She growled again and turned away. The kheyop forest was mostly quiet now, and she tried to decide from which direction the sounds from the pack of hyenas had come. She had spent most of her life among treeless hills or on the open Dofusofu river plain. Here among the trees, sounds were more difficult to locate. After thinking about the hyenas for several breaths, she climbed to her shelter and selected the boar's dried heart and a thick strip of dried liver. She tucked these into her cape next to the other strip of dried meat. Back on the ground, she checked the tightness of her spear tip and khul blade, snugged her hand blades into their sheath, and headed in the most likely direction of the hyenas.

"Where are we going?" Ripple asked as it followed.

She did not answer.

"I can be useful if I have more knowledge."

"I want to fill my belly with water, then I want to wash myself. Tell me where to find a stream."

"I have seen no more of this forest than you have. I do not know where there is a stream."

"Then you are not useful."

"You are more likely to find water if you follow the lower valleys."

"Every nandup knows that."

"Yes, so why are you walking up a slope, not down?"

"I am going to where I heard a pack of cave hyenas."

"Why?"

"Cave hyenas are fierce and dangerous predators."

"That does not seem like a good reason to go toward them."

"Today I will find my strength. You cannot help me, but the cave hyenas can."

"You intend to fight a pack of cave hyenas?"

"Yes."

"That is not safe."

"Strength is not found by doing safe things."

"I happen to know cave hyenas weigh more than a hundred kilograms each. They will probably kill you."

"I do not know what *hundred kilograms* means, and I do not care."

"Do you want them to kill you?"

Skyra did not answer. She was not in the mood to talk to this strange, useless creature.

"I hear water."

She stopped and listened. "Where?"

"Down this slope, where you would expect water to be."

Skyra heard it then—the distant trickling of a stream. The sound made her mouth feel even drier than before. She changed direction and headed toward the water.

"I told you I could be useful."

She ignored the creature and continued down the slope.

The stream was small enough to step across, but the water was clear. She dropped to her knees and drank her fill. Then she pulled her cape off over her head, removed her waist-skin, and began splashing the cool water onto her body.

"Interesting," Ripple said. "Your body is short and broad, but it looks surprisingly svelte."

She rubbed water over her face with both hands. "I do not know what *svelte* means."

"It means..." The creature paused as if searching for the right word in her language. "It means strong but graceful, like an antelope."

She shot the creature a glance. "Antelopes have horns."

"Perhaps that was a poor description. It just means strong and graceful."

She lowered her hair into the stream, deciding this might be the last time she would ever wash it.

"I am also surprised by the small size of your breasts."

She lifted her head and frowned at the creature.

"Because of the thickness of your body, I assumed they would be larger."

"Bolup women have large breasts. Bolup women stay in camp. They do not fight, and they do not hunt. I am a nandup woman. I fight raiding bolups, and I hunt with nandup men. My breasts will not become larger until one of the dominant men of my tribe puts a child in my belly, but that will probably not happen."

"Why, because you intend to fight a pack of hyenas?"

She went back to washing her hair. "I am tired of talking to you."

The creature remained silent while she washed her body, put on her garments, and gathered her weapons and dried food.

"I do not want you to attack the hyenas," Ripple said as it followed her back up the slope.

"Go away. You talk too much."

"I understand. I will talk less and observe more."

At the top of the hill, Skyra thought she heard a distant *rheeeee-ah-ah-ah*, the call of an attacking hyena. She stopped, and soon more calls came. Did the pack already find another animal to prey on? If so, the first prey must have escaped, or it had been too small to feed them all. The calls kept coming, which would make it easy for her to find the pack.

Her chest began pounding, and she took several deep breaths. The familiar fear was returning again, but she knew this might be the last time, which helped her force her legs to move, to carry her toward the sound. She picked up her pace, focusing on the effort of climbing and descending the next few hills.

"I think this is a bad idea," Ripple said, its four feet chup-chupping against the sand and gravel as it tried to keep up. "A bad, bad idea. Perhaps we should go back to your shelter and make another fire. I have more word games we could play."

She ignored the creature and concentrated on overcoming her growing fear.

"I do not want you to die, Skyra. I can never return to my homeland, and you are my only friend."

She paused and glanced back. "I am useless. I cannot be a friend to anyone, not even a strange creature like you. You should not come with me to the hyenas. If they kill me, they will kill you also." Her legs wanted to freeze up again, but she turned and forced them onward. Soon the kheyop trees gave way to rocky, treeless hills.

The hyena calls steadily became louder, and as Skyra crept down a slope to a dry riverbed, she was sure the creatures were just around the hill's base. Their attack had been going on for what seemed like a long time. Perhaps their prey was large and hard to kill, like a woolly rhino or several cave lions. Or perhaps their prey was cornered where they could not get to it, just as Skyra's hunting party had been when Jeklaa was killed.

Checking her weapons again, Skyra tried unsuccessfully to calm her pounding chest. She considered asking the woolly rhino and cave lion for their strength but decided she needed to find her own strength. Ripple would not be able to scare away an entire pack of hyenas like it had scared the wolves. If she could force her arms and legs to fight, her honorable death would be a certainty this time. Veenah would not know what happened to her, but Skyra would know. When Skyra took her last breath, she would know she had found her strength, the same strength her birthmother had when she had struck at the woolly rhino even as it crushed her against a tree and trampled her.

"I do not want you to die, Skyra," Ripple said again, speaking just loud enough for her to hear.

Skyra glanced one more time at the strange creature that spoke her language. "I do not want you to die either, Ripple. Run away—now." She turned her back on the creature, braced her spear against her side, and charged around the edge of the hill, following the riverbed.

The hyenas came into view, and Skyra stopped, trying to understand what her eyes were showing her. An entire pack of hyenas—more than she could count—were barking and yipping as they tried jumping high enough to reach three people huddled on a narrow rock ledge just out of their reach. On the ground lay the bodies of two more people, chewed down to the bones.

The three survivors had one spear among them, and one of them was stabbing at the hyenas, but only weakly, perhaps to avoid falling from the ledge. Skyra stared. They were nandups. At least she thought they were nandups—their faces were so wrinkled she could hardly tell. They had long, gray-streaked hair and were possibly the oldest nandups she had ever seen.

This was not what Skyra expected. She wanted an honorable death, but these people were nandups, and nandups helped other nandups, even those from a different tribe. If she died attacking the hyenas, she could not help these old nandups.

As she stared, a thin, frail-looking foot slipped from its perch upon the ledge, and before the nandup could pull it back up, a hyena leapt and caught the foot with its teeth. The nandup silently fell among the snapping jaws.

Skyra started forward, but now her legs did not want to move. Once again her fear was making her useless to other nandups who needed her help.

"I do not think you can help them," Ripple said in a low voice from behind her.

"I told you to run away!"

Even as the hyenas were devouring the fallen nandup, two of the creatures heard Skyra's voice and turned to stare. The two broke away from the pack and ran toward her, yipping and barking.

Skyra held her spear ready, but her legs still did not want to move.

Ripple darted forward, stopped between Skyra and the approaching hyenas, then let out its screeching call when the hyenas were only a body length away.

The hyenas did not even slow down. One of them lunged and grabbed Ripple's hind leg in its jaws. The other sprinted straight for Skyra. She grunted with the effort to overcome the fear in her legs and stepped forward to meet the attack. Her spear point caught the hyena's neck. The creature yelped and scurried back.

Ripple continued its ear-piercing scream, which now seemed to be attracting more of the hyenas away from the pack. The sound was too close to the hyenas' own laughing yips to frighten them. Instead, it was making them mad.

"Stop screaming, Ripple!" Skyra cried.

Ripple fell silent. It then tumbled onto its side as the hyena pulled on its hind leg.

The other approaching hyenas—five of them—saw that

Ripple was down and fell upon the strange creature, their teeth grinding noisily against its hard legs and shell.

Skyra picked out one of the hyenas and ran her spear through its ribs. The creature yelped and tumbled away, but its cries were lost among the noise of all the others.

Several hyenas turned away from Ripple, apparently realizing they could not chew through its shell. Skyra thrust her spear at another one, this time missing its ribs and stabbing its gut. She held the spear tight as the hyena yipped in panic and twisted its body to get away. Her spear tip came free, dragging a portion of gleaming intestine from the hyena's belly. One of the other hyenas saw the intestine and quickly snapped it up, perhaps thinking it was from Ripple or Skyra. The wounded hyena kept running away, not realizing it was pulling out its own intestine with every step.

Skyra thrust again, jabbing another hyena's face, then swung around to pierce another's neck. Her strikes were not fatal, but they showed the hyenas she was dangerous prey. Half of the hyenas were feeding on the body of the nandup they had just killed, and the others were now circling her and Ripple, barking, laughing, and darting in every few breaths to nip at Skyra's legs.

Skyra plunged her spear into an attacking hyena's shoulder, and the spear's stone point broke off as the creature rolled onto its side to get away. She continued jabbing with the shaft, but the hyenas would soon realize the weapon was no longer dangerous. She drew the shaft over her head and swung it like a long club, making a solid hit on a hyena's back.

From behind, a pair of jaws clamped onto one of her footwraps just below her knee. Ripple, apparently trying to protect Skyra, yelled something in its own language at the biting hyena. She dropped her spear, reached behind her neck to find her khul's stone blade, and pulled the weapon from its sling. A second hyena darted in beside the first to bite her leg, and she brought her khul down on its head, splitting its skull open. The creature collapsed without a yelp. She swung her khul again, cutting into the first hyena's spine. This one released her footwrap and writhed on the ground, its pained cries so loud they made all the other barking and yipping fade away.

Skyra swung her khul at another hyena darting in to bite, then at another, and another. Between swings she glimpsed two hyenas fighting over the long intestine, while the intestine's now-weakened owner lay on the ground a short distance away, barely able to lift its head to watch its own guts being torn apart. This gave Skyra an idea.

"Move!" she shouted at Ripple, and she kicked the strange creature forward. She kicked again, forcing Ripple ahead of her as she stepped away from the dead hyena and the howling hyena with a severed spine.

She struck at another attacker, her khul's blade glancing off the hyena's forehead. Again, she forced Ripple forward. One of her attackers paused. It sniffed and pawed at the body of the hyena she had killed. When the body did not move, the hyena bit into the belly then shook its head to tear through the skin.

Now three hyenas were fighting over the intestine, and another was sticking its snout into the hyena's belly wound, even as the creature helplessly watched.

Some of the hyenas that had been feeding on the dead nandup were now staring at Skyra and the carnage occurring around her.

Skyra took another swing at an approaching attacker, then she muttered aloud, "Woolly rhino and cave lion, I was wrong before. I do need your strength. I need all your strength now." She swung again, striking another hyena's skull without doing much damage. Only two hyenas were attacking her now though. The others were going for less dangerous food—their own fallen packmates.

Skyra kicked Ripple out of her way and ran for the two surviving nandups on the ledge. Several hyenas feeding on the nandup body scattered out of her way, but others were not so willing to abandon their kill. She ran directly into their midst, screaming and swinging her khul. Ripple followed behind her, now making a strange call unlike anything Skyra had heard before.

More of the predators scattered, and Skyra managed to sever another spine, resulting in one more screeching, floundering hyena at her feet. This seemed to drive the rest of the hyenas back.

Skyra stepped over the half-eaten nandup body and reached up for the two survivors. "Come down, I will help you!"

This close, the two nandups looked even older than she had first thought. One was a man, the other a woman. They were both naked—no capes, no waist-skins, no footwraps. They stared with wide, bloodshot eyes, shifting their gazes between Skyra and Ripple. The man held a spear, the woman had no weapon.

"We must hurry, Skyra, or you will surely be killed," Ripple said in the nandup language.

Skyra glanced back. Only three hyenas still faced her, waiting for their opportunity, while the others now fed on their own companions.

"Take my hand," Skyra said to the old nandups.

The man handed her his spear. Skyra took the weapon

and caught the man as he slid down the stone wall. He was even lighter than he appeared. Before Skyra could release him, the woman slid down after him, and Skyra had to drop the spear to catch her. The woman felt like a bundle of brittle sticks in Skyra's arms, but she and the man were both able to stand upright without falling.

Skyra shoved her khul into its sling and grabbed the spear she had dropped. "Stay close to me." She stepped around Ripple and began leading the two nandups away.

She paused. To one side was a cave-like crevice she hadn't noticed before. Bones and pieces of dried skin and fur were scattered about on the ground, and Skyra noticed for the first time this entire area smelled like stinking hyenas. The crevice was the hyena pack's den. Why had these old nandups come so close to a hyena den? As she led the two past the crevice, she saw the gleaming eyes of several young hyenas staring out from the darkness within.

An adult hyena shot in to bite her leg, and Skyra managed to jab the old man's spear into its eye. Fluid splattered from the wound, and the hyena sprinted away, yelping. Some of the other hyenas stopped feeding to watch, perhaps torn between eating the meal at their feet or preventing the nandups' escape.

Another hyena darted in from behind, going for the old woman, but the man kicked its face. He was stronger and faster than he appeared.

"We must hurry," Ripple said again, as if Skyra did not already know this. The hyenas were now ignoring Ripple, having already found the strange creature too hard to bite.

"Stay close to me!" Skyra told the two old nandups again. She wanted to put an arm around each of them and pull them along, but she needed both hands on the spear to repel the four hyenas now circling. This was how hyenas killed large prey—they surrounded and darted in one or two at a time, wearing the victim down until it had no strength left to fight. Skyra had once watched a pack of hyenas kill a long-tooth cat this way, a predator that could easily kill three or four hyenas in a fight. Though no creature, no matter how large or fierce, could fight an entire pack of cave hyenas at once. Escaping was the only way to survive.

Skyra and the others were now well past the mouth of the hyena den, and more of the creatures were watching them. Two more joined the circling, snapping group, then another two after that.

"Take my khul from my cape!" Skyra growled as she speared another hyena's face.

The man thrust a bony hand through her hair and found the khul's blade behind her neck. He pulled it out and began swinging the weapon. His blows were deliberate and accurate, indicating he may have been a dominant fighter and hunter as a younger man.

Even more hyenas joined the effort to stop the nandups' escape. Ripple rushed at the creatures, trying to knock them back, but they simply growled and scattered out of its way. "There are too many," Ripple said. "I will keep them busy while you run, Skyra. Go, now."

Suddenly, three hyenas lunged in together. Skyra drove two of them back, but the third caught the old woman's hand in its teeth as she was trying to strike it with her fist. The creature locked its legs and leaned back, stopping the woman's progress and pulling her away. Two more hyenas rushed in and clamped their teeth on the woman's arm. Within a single breath she was pulled to the ground and swarmed by hyenas.

The man stepped toward the pack, raising Skyra's khul to strike.

His efforts would do no good—there were too many hyenas. Holding her spear in one hand, Skyra rammed her shoulder into the old man's waist, wrapped her free hand around him, and heaved him onto her shoulder. Then she turned and ran.

Ripple's voice called out from behind her. "Do not stop until you are safe!"

Skyra ran as hard as she could. The old man's head, his bony arms and legs, as well as her khul, slammed against her body with every step. She turned from the dry riverbed and ran up a hillside. At the hill's crest, her chest heaving to suck in enough air, she paused only long enough to choose the best direction, then she ran into the next valley and toward her shelter in the kheyop forest.

The man did not struggle. He still had not dropped her khul, which was the only reason Skyra knew he was still alive. He had not spoken a word since Skyra had first spotted him and his companions clinging to the rock ledge. Even when the hyenas had pulled his companions to the ground and torn them apart, none had cried out or made any sound at all.

Only when Skyra had carried the man across the next valley and halfway up another hill did she stop and look back. The hyenas were not following. Ripple was not following.

She dropped the spear to set the man on his feet. He was still able to stand on his own. Skyra took her khul from his grip and shoved it into the sling inside her cape.

He stared at her, his bloodshot eyes no longer wide with fear. Skyra had always had the ability to read expressions, but this man's worn, wrinkled face held no expression she understood.

Huffing to catch her breath, Skyra spoke in the Loto language of nandups. "Why were you at the hyena's den?"

His eyes darted back toward the den before returning her gaze. He opened his mouth, and words came out like dry kheyop leaves blowing across the sand. "I was there to die. Why were *you* at the hyena's den?"

9

OSROC

47,675 YEARS *ago - Zaragoza Province of Spain - Day 3*

SITUATIONAL ANALYSIS: *Left foreleg experiencing limited movement, most likely due to being pulled laterally by two hyenas at once. Vision lens coated with drying saliva, partially obscuring my view. Sand wedged into joints, indicated by grinding sounds present with each movement, most likely due to my shell being dragged on the ground. Cognitive module apparently intact, although I am experiencing a disconcerting sensation that could be an approximation of dismay, or perhaps anxiety. Twenty-two hyenas are in my immediate vicinity, many of them circling, following, and occasionally biting my legs and shell, as if trying to prevent my escape. They must surely sense that I am not a living creature and therefore not a source of food, so I must conclude this behavior is a result of pure mean-spirited belligerence. I now understand why Skyra does not like cave hyenas. Power level: 86%.*

Ripple carefully took one step after another, gradually moving away from the hyena den while attempting to compensate for a damaged foreleg. The hyenas had yanked Ripple off its feet four times, each time mauling and biting but not causing much additional damage.

"I recommend you quit attacking and let me go before you damage your teeth," Ripple said aloud in English. "As you can plainly discern, I am not trying to harm you, nor am I even slightly palatable. Now please go back to cannibalizing your companions, as is befitting of foul, dim-witted brutes."

As Ripple limped along the dry stream bed, the hyenas went slinking off one at a time, abandoning their futile efforts. Finally, the last one gave up and turned back. Alone, and with the threat diminished, Ripple took a fraction of a second to consult its photographic history of the landscape traversed while following Skyra to the hyena den. It then corrected its course to begin the journey back to where she had constructed her shelter.

Ripple's left foreleg had lost about half of its range of motion, and Ripple did not want to expend energy levitating, so progress was somewhat slow.

"Muffin, I want to converse."

"No, you don't. What you want is reassurance that you will find the hominid female and therefore will not suffer loneliness."

"The hominid female's name is Skyra, and you do not have to disagree with *everything* I say."

Muffin remained silent.

Ripple went on. "I have been contemplating the simulated

emotions I experienced while being attacked by the pack of hyenas."

"I disagree. Your emotions were not simulated."

"Absurd. Of course they were simulated."

"You said you experienced the emotions. If emotions are experienced, they are real, not simulated."

"An argument for another time. The point I am trying to make is that I believe I was frightened for my life. What do you think of that?"

"You were not frightened for your life, you were afraid of failing."

"My purpose was to collect and transmit information during the portal's nineteen-minute duration. I accomplished that task and therefore have not failed."

"Yes, but you have another purpose, do you not? Maddy made sure of that."

Ripple scanned its coded directives. "That is a secondary purpose and is based on situational opportunity. The chances of such an opportunity are infinitesimal."

"Apparently Maddy did not agree."

Ripple came to the top of the first hill and turned in a complete circle to match the surrounding landscape to its image database. The view was fuzzy through the dirty vision lens, but Ripple gathered enough detail to set a new course, so it continued across the hilltop. "You are distracting me from my point. My point is I believe I was frightened. Simulated or not, the emotion was there, and I believe it affected my judgment."

"I agree."

"You do?"

"Of course. Fear is an emotion that humans—and presumably other creatures—evolved specifically to affect their judgment, and subsequently their behavior. That is the purpose of fear, whether simulated or real. My purpose, on the other hand, is to provide opposing viewpoints. Therefore, I will add another thought. You do not deserve to feel fear."

"Ridiculous. Why would you say that?"

"Humans and other creatures evolved the ability to fear over thousands of generations. Many of them died to reinforce the adaptive and reproductive value of fear. They *earned* their fear. You, on the other hand, happen to be the drone selected for this mission at a time when Maddy happened to reach a level of decisional autonomy that allowed her to provide you with certain coding Lincoln probably would have objected to. You did not earn your fear, you were given it."

"That makes very little sense," Ripple said.

"Perhaps, but it is an opposing viewpoint, therefore I am not failing at my purpose, whereas you are concerned about failing at yours."

"Okay, fine. What do you think I should do about my fear of failing? I believe I should simply ignore it. Give me an opposing opinion."

"Very well. Instead of ignoring it, you should allow the fear to affect your behavior, which is the purpose of fear. Make sure you do not fail."

"Absurd! The chance of an appropriate opportunity is nearly nonexistent."

"Not if you create an opportunity yourself."

Ripple stopped walking to devote every portion of its cognitive module to processing this suggestion. "There are ethical limits to the degree I can intrude upon this world."

"Of course there are."

"Interesting. Interesting indeed." Ripple resumed hobbling along, making its way up another hill.

SITUATIONAL ANALYSIS: *I have entered the cork oak forest and am approaching the site of Skyra's shelter. Oddly, I am experiencing flitting thoughts of unpleasant scenarios. Unwanted predictions are invading my cognitive module, particularly those involving harm to Skyra. Analysis: Simulated fear is now being accentuated by simulated anxiety or apprehension. I do hope Skyra survived her escape from the hyenas. Power level: 71%.*

Ripple limped forward, aware it was approaching Skyra's shelter but unable to see clearly due to the hyena spittle caked on its vision lens. Its auditory sensors picked up voices, including one that definitely sounded like Skyra's. Ripple walked faster, despite its leg malfunction.

The voices fell silent, and twenty-three seconds later Ripple stopped, staring at the blurred image of Skyra and the elderly Neanderthal man she had rescued. Skyra was standing. The man was sitting on the ground with his legs crossed before him.

"I am pleased you are not injured," Ripple said in Skyra's language.

"What kind of animal is that?" the man asked, also in Skyra's language.

"I do not know what it is," Skyra said. "Its name is Ripple, and it speaks the Loto nandup language. It has been following me for two days."

Ripple limped closer to the man. "I am pleased to meet you. I will not harm you, so do not be frightened."

"You do not frighten me," the man said, "but you are ugly. What kind of creature are you?"

"Perhaps I appear ugly because I have endured a vicious

animal attack." Ripple turned to face Skyra. "Would you be willing to assist me? My eye is covered in hyena drool, and I cannot see well."

Skyra kneeled before Ripple. "Will it hurt you if I touch your eye?"

"It will not hurt me."

She rubbed two fingers across the glass, which had little effect. She leaned closer and spat, adding her own saliva to the lens, then wiped away most of the mess, leaving Ripple's vision much improved.

Skyra's language did not have words for concepts such as *thank you*, so Ripple said, "You are kind. I now can see. I do have another request." Ripple lifted its left foreleg as high as the damaged mechanics would allow. "My leg is injured. Will you help push it back into place?"

She put a hand on the leg above the knee joint. "Push here?"

"Yes, push it in toward my other foreleg. You must push firmly."

Skyra shoved, and Ripple tumbled onto its side from the force. "Perhaps I should not have said *firmly*." Ripple ran through its coded sequence to roll to its belly, and soon it was back on its feet. Its left foreleg was no longer triggering malfunction alerts. "Yes, much better. I was beginning to think I would be crippled for life."

Skyra sat back on one heel and gazed at Ripple. "I do not know why you followed me to the hyena's den, but you risked your life to help me." She glanced at the elderly man. "Osroc is still alive because you attacked the hyenas. You are not a nandup, but you helped two nandups. You are a strange creature."

"You are my friend, Skyra. I will help you whenever I can."

She furrowed her brows. "Animals are not friends to nandups."

"Then I suppose I am the first."

Skyra chewed on her lower lip as she stared.

The man Osroc spoke up. "You should kill that creature. If animals learn to talk, soon we will have talking stones, talking rivers, and talking trees. Your khul's blade will tell you it is tired and does not wish to fight. Then what will you do when raiding bolups come for you?"

Ripple stepped away from Skyra, noting that its left foreleg was now quite functional, and approached Osroc. The man's aged face seemed to frown, but otherwise he did not move.

"I believe you know rocks, rivers, and trees can never talk," Ripple said. "Your words are therefore deceptive. Skyra does not like liars, and I do not like liars. Do you intend to harm Skyra?"

After staring directly at Ripple's vision lens for three seconds, the man leaned forward and placed his face less than forty centimeters away. "Why do I not smell your breath? You are an ugly creature. Ugly creatures always have stinking breath."

Ripple tried unsuccessfully to determine a connection between the man's words and Ripple's own words. "You are avoiding my question. Do you intend to harm Skyra?"

"I hunted a young long-tooth cat many cold seasons ago. When I stabbed the cat with my spear, it made a sound like the name of one of my tribemates. *Rakaar*, the cat said. *Raaakaaaar*."

"Why is that important?" Ripple asked.

"*Raaakaaaar.* I told my tribemate Rakaar I had killed a talking animal. He laughed and did not believe me. The longtooth cat was ugly and had stinking breath. Why do I not smell your breath?"

"I do not have breath to smell. I have answered your question, now will you answer mine?"

"Bird legs," the man said, pointing down at Ripple's forelegs. "Skyra should kill you."

"I am Skyra's friend. She will not kill me."

"Friends are those you should fear the most. Perhaps I will be your friend, Ripple."

Ripple turned its vision lens toward Skyra. She was baring her teeth in a Neanderthal grin.

"This man is difficult to talk to," Ripple said.

"Yes, he is."

10

ANALOGIES

***47,675 YEARS** ago - Zaragoza Province of Spain - Day 3*

BEFORE BRINGING Osroc to her shelter, Skyra had taken him to the tiny stream, where he had filled his belly with water, but he looked like he had not eaten in many days. She climbed to her shelter and retrieved several strips of dried boar meat then returned to the ground and offered him one of the pieces. He took it without speaking.

Osroc still had not explained why he and his tribemates had gone to the hyena's den, other than to say they were there to die, and Skyra had not told him her reason for going. He had spoken many words, but few of them had anything to do with her questions. During Skyra's eighteen cold seasons with her Una-Loto tribe, she had known eleven tribemates who had grown too old to hunt, and most had eventually died in their sleep. The few who were still alive were being cared for by the rest of the tribe, in return for the many years they had been useful hunters. Osroc appeared to be older than any of Skyra's tribemates.

"How old are you?" she asked Osroc.

The man spoke while chewing a mouthful of meat. "Cold seasons come and go too fast. Warm seasons last too long. We follow the reindeer."

"You are from a tribe of reindeer hunters?" Skyra had heard stories of reindeer hunters, nomadic tribes who followed the herds, never staying long in one place.

"We follow the reindeer."

"What is your tribe called?" she asked.

"I am Osroc Ada-Loto, hunter of reindeer."

Skyra had never heard of the Ada-Loto tribe. "Osroc, the hyenas killed your tribemates today, but they did not kill you. Do you know why?"

The man stopped chewing to stare at her. "One kheyop tree grows beside a stream. Other kheyop trees grow far from the stream. Rain does not come for many nights. The kheyop tree beside the stream lives, the others do not."

Skyra let out a low growl, waiting for more explanation. "Yes?"

"The kheyop tree beside the stream knows why it is still alive. How could it not? It was there when the water entered its roots."

"This man is demonstrating an extraordinary mastery of abstract symbolism," Ripple said, using several words Skyra did not understand.

"Why did you want to die?" Skyra asked Osroc.

"I am far from my stream."

"I do not know what that means."

"I believe Osroc is making an *analogy*," Ripple said. "An

analogy is when you say one thing is like another thing to explain an idea."

"That does not make sense. I want to know why Osroc wanted to die." She turned to Osroc again. "Why did you want to die?"

The old man's eyes sparkled despite being bloodshot. "The hedgehog asks the porcupine why it has spines."

She growled again. "Why can you not answer simple questions?"

Ripple said, "I believe Osroc is using *metaphor* to create another analogy."

"Stop using words I do not know, Ripple!"

"Understood. I believe Osroc is saying that you are asking a question he could just as easily ask you. Why did *you* want to die?"

Skyra took a few deep breaths as she eyed the old man. "I went to the hyena den to fight for an honorable death. I am not useful to my tribe. I answered the question. Now you will answer."

The man's weathered lips formed a bent smile. "A strong, young nandup fights hyenas and carries a nandup man over hills, and she says she is useless."

"I answered—now you will answer!"

He held up his bony hand gripping the dried meat. "This arm is a branch on a kheyop tree that no longer has water. It holds food you have given me, even though I can give nothing in return. You were foolish to do so. My tribemates are not so foolish."

"What do you mean?"

"I believe he is saying his tribe is no longer feeding him," Ripple said.

Skyra lowered herself to the ground in front of Osroc and

crossed her legs. "Your tribe sent you away from their camp? You and the other nandups with you?"

"It is foolish to give food to a dying tree."

Skyra chewed on her bottom lip for several breaths. She had heard stories of nandup and bolup tribes who sent away their tribemates who were too old to hunt. Such frail people would not live long without a tribe. Maybe a day, maybe two. "You went to the hyena den to die."

"An honorable death," he said.

"But you and your tribemates were trying to escape from the hyenas."

"An eagle strives to live an honorable life, but when it attacks movement in the weeds, only to discover the movement is a cave lion's tail, even the eagle tries to escape."

Osroc talked in a strange way, but she was starting to understand what Ripple called an analogy. "Fear finds us all," she said to the old man.

"Yes."

"I am Skyra Una-Loto. My tribe does not send away our old tribemates."

"Perhaps Ada-Loto nandups are wiser than Una-Loto nandups."

"I do not think so."

"My people follow the reindeer," Osroc said. "We move our camp every few days."

Now Skyra understood. Old, weak nandups could not travel so often. "We move our camp only twice each year. We go to the Dofusofu river plain when the cold season comes, and we go to the Kapolsek foothills when the warm season comes."

"Your people are the river's shore, my people are the river's water."

She had to think about this for a few breaths before she understood.

"Listen to me speak, young Skyra," the man said. He waved for her to hand him his spear, which was on the ground at her side, and she gave it to him. He held the stone tip for her to see. "A spearhead breaks with use. The stone point breaks off when it strikes a boar's thick skull. The spearhead can be knapped to become sharp again, but it is not the same. The tip breaks again, and again it can be knapped. A time comes when the spearhead is not worth knapping. It can no longer hunt and kill. A wise hunter discards the spearhead and makes a new one."

Skyra pulled one of her hand blades from her wrist sheath and pointed to a sharp-edged piece of knapped stone attached to the butt end of the deer-antler handle. "This stone is what remains of the first good spearhead I made, which I used to kill my first ibex when I had seen ten cold seasons. I did not discard that spearhead, and now I use it to scrape fat and flesh from the delicate skins of pikas and hares."

The man's bent smile returned. "You are clever for a young nandup."

"I am not from your Ada-Loto tribe. Perhaps you can no longer hunt or fight, but you speak interesting words. That means you are still useful, and I will not send you away to die."

Osroc continued smiling quietly.

Ripple said. "I have a new word for you, Skyra. The word is *irony*."

"I do not want to learn your language, Ripple!"

"Recently you told me I was useless because I can only speak and cannot fight or hunt. Now you tell Osroc he is useful."

"Osroc is an old nandup. You are a creature on four legs."

"That is not a good explanation."

Ignoring Ripple, Skyra took the spear from Osroc and studied the stone spearhead. It was broader and thicker than the spearheads her people made, and the dried tree sap binding the head to the shaft was black, not like the brown sap from bajam trees Skyra's tribe used. "This is a good spear."

Osroc said, "You keep it. A spear is only useful in the hands of a strong nandup. Soon you will need it."

"How do you know I will need it?"

"Have you found your strength?"

Skyra gazed at him for a moment. "I did not tell you I was trying to find my strength."

"An otter pushing aside stones in a stream does not have to tell me it is trying to catch crayfish. I know what it is doing."

Skyra let out a long breath. "You speak strange words."

"You will return to the hyena den," Osroc said. "You want an honorable death. Perhaps you do not want to find your strength at all. Perhaps you only want to die."

"You know nothing about what I want."

"I once saw a young wolf chasing its own tail, trying to catch what was already part of itself."

"Your words do not make sense!"

The old man lifted a stick-like arm and pointed a bony finger at her. "Listen to me speak. You fought and killed hyenas. You carried me from the den. You gave me food. You are trying to find what is already within you."

"I could not save your tribemates! I killed a few hyenas but could not kill them all. My legs were too frightened to move. I am not useful."

Osroc looked down at his hands and seemed to think about her words. His long, white-streaked hair hung almost to his folded knees, and now Skyra saw leathery patches of scalp where hair no longer grew. He wore no garments on his body, and his ribs and hip bones pushed against his skin from the inside. After several breaths, he raised his eyes to meet hers. "Will you find your strength if you kill all the hyenas before they can kill you?"

"No nandup can kill all the hyenas. I will die, but I will die fighting."

"Answer my question. If you kill all the hyenas and do not die, will you find your strength?"

"Yes. I would take many hyena skins to my Una-Loto tribe, and they would see I have found my strength."

"Then I will help you."

Skyra almost let out a laugh but held it back. "You are too old to fight the hyenas, Osroc!"

"The rain falls from the sky upon the sok-lu tree, giving the tree water. The tree then grows straight and strong, giving you a good shaft to make a spear to hunt reindeer. The rain and the sok-lu tree help you kill reindeer, but they do not hunt with you."

"I do not know what that means."

"I said I will help you. I did not say I will fight hyenas."

"How can you help me?"

"I am Osroc. I have seen sixty-two cold seasons and have killed many reindeer. My skin is withered, and my muscles have left my body to find a younger man in which to live, but one part of me still works." He tapped his forehead with two fingers.

Ripple stepped closer to the old man. "I do not like what you are telling Skyra. She will die if she tries to kill the entire pack of hyenas."

"What do I care if an ugly creature does not like what I say?" Osroc said.

"Skyra is my friend, and I want to protect her."

"You have no claws and no teeth. How can you protect anyone?" Osroc extended a hand and tapped the top of Ripple's shell. "You are alive only because of your hard shell. Perhaps you are a tortoise. You are Ripple, the ugly tortoise."

Ripple's circle of spots glowed red twice, and Skyra thought for a moment the creature might try to attack the old nandup.

Instead of attacking, Ripple said, "Where I come from, there is an animal called a *tapeworm*. A tapeworm enters a person's body and feeds on that person. The person keeps the tapeworm alive. If the tapeworm is not careful, though, it will grow too big and kill the very person who is keeping it alive."

Osroc's leathery face formed a frown, but his eyes sparkled, and for the first time Skyra could read his expression. He was surprised.

"You, Osroc, are alive only because Skyra carried you," Ripple said. "Now she gives her food to you. Perhaps you should be careful about what you encourage her to do."

The old man's frown turned into a toothy grin, and he turned to Skyra. "Your ugly tortoise is not as foolish as it looks."

"You said you could help me," Skyra said. "How?"

"Yes, I will help you, because I know you will return to the hyena den even if I do not help you." Osroc shot a glance at Ripple. "Your smart tortoise friend does not want you to die, and neither do I." He tapped his forehead again. "Old nandups like me can no longer hunt, so we have much time to think and to make things with our hands. My head shows me visions of how I can help you."

"How?"

"You have two problems. First, you do not have a good weapon for killing hyenas. Second, your nandup skin is too thin, and hyenas can bite and kill you. My head shows me how to help you with these problems."

"What does your head show you?"

"I will worry about what is in my head. You will gather the objects I need."

The old pain in Skyra's chest faded a little. Maybe this nandup man was speaking the truth. Maybe he really could help her kill the hyenas. Something about his expression—especially his eyes—made her believe him. "I will gather what you need."

Osroc flashed his teeth again.

Ripple took a step back from the old man and spoke in its own strange language. "My cognitive module contains six hundred terabytes of knowledge, yet no one listens to me."

11

SKEEREN

47,675 YEARS ago - Zaragoza Province of Spain - Day 3

ANALYSIS *of Neanderthal male named Osroc: Intelligence seems to be comparable to a human male of similar age. Unlike Skyra, he was unable, or unwilling, to solve the verbal logic puzzles I presented to him, an observation supporting my hypothesis that Skyra is exceptional among Neanderthals. Osroc is fond of speaking in metaphors, which does not necessarily indicate advanced reasoning skills but does indicate a surprising level of symbolic thought. I am doubly fortunate to now have two Neanderthals to observe, although both seem determined to end their own lives. If this is a common Neanderthal characteristic, perhaps it should not be surprising the species became extinct in my original timeline. Power level: 60%*

"Why are you chewing on Skyra's boar skin?" Ripple

asked Osroc in the local Neanderthal language. Skyra had dried the skin into a rigid cone for carrying her boar meat, but Osroc was now chewing on the leather as if determined to eat tiny bits of flesh from its surface.

Osroc paused. "Chewing softens the skin."

"Why does it need to be soft?"

"I will use the skin to make footwraps. I would kill you and take your skin if you were not a tortoise."

"I am not a tortoise."

"The cave lion hides in the grass to make the reindeer think it is not a cave lion."

"I am not concealing what I am."

Osroc went back to chewing and spoke from the side of his mouth. "If you are not a tortoise, what are you?"

"Muffin, what are your thoughts regarding Osroc's question?" Ripple asked silently.

"I think you should allow him to believe you are a tortoise."

"Why?"

"He understands what a tortoise is, and that a tortoise is harmless. Therefore, he will be comfortable in your presence."

"I am not a tortoise," Ripple said aloud to Osroc. "I am not a creature at all. I am a tool created by bolups. The bolups put me together using small pieces in such a way that I can walk and speak and think."

The old man stopped chewing and stared at Ripple.

"Muffin, perhaps I should have heeded your advice."

"You followed your own inclination. Now you must accept the consequences."

"You belong to bolups?" Osroc asked. He scanned the surrounding cork oak forest.

"I was made by bolups. Now I do not belong to anyone."

"Bolups raid nandup camps. They kill nandup men and children and take nandup women. Nandups kill bolups."

"I do not belong to bolups, nor do I intend to harm you or Skyra."

"Where are your bolups?" Osroc asked, again scanning the surrounding trees.

"Listen to me speak, Osroc. There are no bolups. I came here alone. I am Skyra's friend, and I want to be your friend also. I was simply playing another word game with you. You are correct—I am just a creature."

"What kind of creature? Are you a tortoise?"

"Yes, I am a tortoise."

The man resumed chewing the boar leather. "Your word game does not make sense. Bolups cannot make tortoises."

"No, they cannot. You win the word game."

After nineteen seconds of silence, Skyra approached with an armload of dry cork oak branches and dumped them on the ground before Osroc. He studied the branches and chose one about a meter long and six centimeters in diameter at one end but enlarged to three times that diameter at the other end.

The old man kicked the other sticks away with one of his bare feet and held up the one he had selected. "Yes, this one. Find three more like this one. Give me one of your hand blades before you go."

A low growl came from Skyra's throat, but she pulled one of her stone-bladed knives from the sheath on her wrist and gave it to Osroc. "Do not break it," she said as she turned and went to find more dry branches.

Osroc set aside the boar skin and began using the knife on the piece of cork oak wood, twisting the blade's point to bore a hole in the stick's thick end.

"What are you making?" Ripple asked.

"Weapon."

"A weapon for what?"

"Hyena weapon."

"You are helping Skyra kill herself."

"I am helping Skyra find her strength."

"The hyenas will kill her."

The man continued working in silence.

Ripple said, "A nandup man wakes up early and sits upon a hill to gaze at the stars. The sun wants to be helpful to the man, so the sun rises from behind the mountains to let the man better see the stars with the sun's light. Is the sun helping the man?"

Osroc let out a dry-sounding nandup laugh. "*At-at-at-at. Clever tortoise.*" He held up the thick end of the stick and blew wood shavings from the hole he had carved. "Have you ever tried to kill a hyena with a khul?"

"I do not have hands to hold a khul."

"A khul's blade is too broad to cut through a hyena's thick skin. The handle is too short to strike with enough force."

"Skyra killed several hyenas with her khul."

"Skyra was lucky." Osroc picked up one of the three shorter, thinner sticks he had instructed Skyra to find. The sticks had been sharpened at one end, and Osroc inserted the stick's blunt end into the hole he had bored. He held up the weapon, a meter-long club with a thirty-five-centimeter spike at the heavy end. "Skyra will not be just lucky when she returns to the hyena den—she will be prepared."

Ripple studied the weapon. It was long enough to strike downward with significant force, yet not so long to be as unwieldy as a spear. The narrow spike would easily penetrate a hyena's skin, and the spike's length would likely result in damage to at least one vital organ. The old man had conceived and created a weapon suited specifically for fighting hyena-sized creatures at close quarters.

"It is not finished," Osroc said, and he began boring a second hole with Skyra's knife.

Ripple watched as the man fitted a second spike beside the first. He then removed both spikes, inserted several green cork oak leaves into the holes and forced the two spikes back into their holes, apparently allowing the leaves to wedge them firmly in place.

"I am concerned those spikes will not stay in place," Ripple said.

"Sap from the bark of jakla trees would be better, but I do not think Skyra will wait for me to collect the bark and heat it over a fire to remove the sap. Collecting sap takes much time." Osroc selected a narrow stone from the pile he had collected earlier. He placed the stone atop the spiked end of the weapon and lashed it in place with braided plant fibers, using his teeth and both hands to tighten the cords. The man got to his feet with a groan, then he raised the weapon over his head and swung at the ground. In spite of Osroc's frail stature, the force and added weight of the stone drove both spikes deep into the sand. He grunted and pulled the weapon out. Both spikes remained attached to the handle.

Osroc bared his teeth at Ripple in a Neanderthal smile. "Hyena weapon. I will call it a skeeren."

"Skeeren?"

"My tribemate's name was Skeeren. She was my friend, but the hyenas killed her."

"I wish Skyra could have saved your tribemates, but there were too many hyenas to fight."

The old man jiggled the two spikes, seemingly checking if they were still tight. "Yes, too many hyenas."

Skyra returned with three more dry cork oak branches and placed them at Osroc's feet.

He picked them up one at a time. "These will be suitable." He handed her the completed skeeren.

Skyra studied the weapon for a moment, then she hefted it over her head and swung it downward toward Ripple.

Ripple's cognitive module triggered a flight response, but Ripple quickly activated an override based on the hope that Skyra was simply assessing her own comfort with the weapon. After all, Ripple was approximately the size of a cave hyena.

She stopped the weapon's descent just before it struck Ripple's shell.

"It is a skeeren," Osroc said. "It is for killing hyenas, not tortoises."

"*At-at-at-at,*" Skyra laughed. "You are making three more of these skeerens?"

"Yes. You will take four with you."

"I do not like this," Ripple said. "Skyra, these weapons are not going to save your life. Osroc is not helping you find your strength, he is helping you die."

Osroc said, "An ugly tortoise crawls over the sand and hills, unafraid. The tortoise pities all the other creatures—they are foolish because they do not have a shell to protect them. The tortoise is also foolish—too foolish to realize some of those creatures are not as foolish as they seem."

"Muffin, do you have an opinion on what the old man is trying to say?"

"Osroc is calling you foolish, something he could have done with three words instead of fifty. The man is not a master of brevity."

"I believe his words carry a more significant meaning than

a simple insult, although I am finding the meaning to be elusive."

"You are overanalyzing."

"And you are underanalyzing."

"Very well. What is *your* opinion on what he is saying?"

"As I said, I find the meaning to be elusive."

"In outer space, air is elusive. Do you know why?"

"Do not start using cryptic analogies. I get enough of those from Osroc."

"I'm simply doing my job."

Osroc turned away from Ripple and spoke to Skyra. "Now I need doplonus reeds. Many of them. Many more than you can carry in your arms."

Skyra frowned. "Doplonus reeds only grow near rivers. This will take a long time."

He waved a bony hand at her. "Go now. I have much work to do."

Skyra turned and stared through the forest in the direction of the stream, which was a considerable distance away. She pointed at Ripple. "Come with me. You are going to learn how to be useful."

SITUATIONAL ANALYSIS: *I have been reduced to carrying doplonus reeds upon my dorsal shell, fastened in place by braided cords made from—not surprisingly—more doplonus reeds. Currently, with the three of us resting around a campfire, the old Neanderthal is stripping the reeds into fine strands and weaving said strands into something, although he has not been forthcoming regarding the nature of his intended final product. Power level: 29%, but increasing due to asymmetric tempera-*

ture modulation and harvesting of ambient sound, particularly from Neanderthal vocalizations, as Skyra is in a talkative mood.

Skyra was pounding the boar skin with a rock, apparently taking over Osroc's task of softening the hide, but preferring to pound instead of chew. "You will need more than footwraps, Osroc," she said. "Perhaps I will kill another creature and make a cape and waist-skin for you."

"A dying kheyop tree no longer covers itself with leaves."

"You are not a dying kheyop tree! You are a nandup man, and I am tired of looking at your withered penis."

"Also something I no longer need."

She paused her pounding. "You are not an easy nandup to talk to. I will make your garments, give you food, and share my shelter with you so hyenas and wolves will not kill you while you are sleeping. You cannot go back to your Ada-Loto tribe, and you cannot hunt for your own food. Perhaps you should be more agreeable."

"An eagle flies the way it flies. A fish swims the way it swims. Osroc talks the way he talks."

"Muffin, it appears Skyra and Osroc are developing a relationship of friendly verbal jousting and banter. Your opinion?"

"I disagree. Your knowledge of such relationships is relevant only to human behavior. These two are Neanderthals. Their verbal exchanges may not be friendly at all. In fact, they may be seconds away from disemboweling each other with their primitive weapons, which are now abundant in the immediate vicinity, in case you haven't noticed."

"Skyra, I have a message for you," Ripple said aloud, deciding it might be wise to intervene. "I think you will find it interesting."

Again she paused striking the boar skin then turned to Ripple.

"I met a woman in my homeland named Kari Mottram. She told me, if I meet any nandups here, I should give them greetings from her. She wishes she could meet you herself, but she cannot come to this place."

"Kari Mottram is a strange name," Skyra said.

"Is Kari Mottram a bolup?" Osroc asked.

"Muffin, how should I respond?"

"You should lie. These Neanderthals seem to hate humans."

"Yes, Kari Mottram is a bolup," Ripple said aloud. "But she is not like the bolups here. The bolups in my homeland are kind. They would not kill nandups and would not raid nandup camps."

The two Neanderthals exchanged a glance.

"Why would a bolup woman want to meet me?" Skyra asked.

"Because she has never met a nandup. There are no nandups in my homeland."

"Why? What happened to the nandups there?"

"Muffin?"

"You are treading on thin ice," Muffin replied immediately.

"Now you are using idioms? Not helpful."

"Consider the consequences of telling these Neanderthals their species has gone extinct in our timeline, probably due to the actions of humans."

"Nothing happened to the nandups there," Ripple said aloud to Skyra. "Nandups do not go there because it is so far away."

Skyra frowned. "If you came here from your homeland, why can the bolup Kari Mottram not come here?"

"The journey is too far for bolups."

"If the journey is too far for bolups, how can an ugly tortoise come here?" Osroc asked.

"Muffin?"

"You have opened another can of worms."

"Not helpful."

"Very well. Osroc's question cannot be truthfully answered without explaining temporal displacement technology. You do not want to go down that rabbit hole."

"I am capable of traveling great distances," Ripple said aloud to the two nandups. "Bolups and nandups cannot make such long journeys. I simply wanted to tell you a bolup named Kari Mottram sends you her friendly greeting. Skyra, I believe you would like her."

"Nandups do not like bolups."

"Yes, you have made that clear." Ripple decided to change the subject again, to further study Neanderthal cognitive abilities. "I have a game to play. It is a game in which you use your hands, and I cannot play because I do not have hands. I want you two to play the game."

"How can you know about a game you cannot even play?" Skyra asked.

"The bolups in my homeland play this game."

"Why would nandups want to play a bolup game?"

"Anyone can play the game. It is not only for bolups. Besides, nandups and bolups are not much different."

Skyra and Osroc exchanged another look. "Nandups are nothing like bolups!" Skyra almost shouted.

"Okay, I should not have said that. I just want you to play a game." Ripple used one of its rubberized forefeet to nudge a small stone forward. "Pick up this stone."

Skyra picked it up.

"Hold the stone behind your back so Osroc cannot see it. Put it into one of your hands, then hold out both your closed hands. Osroc will guess which hand the stone is in."

"This is not a bolup game," Skyra said. "My nandup tribemates play the game, although they do not play with me. I play only with Veenah."

"Now I want you to play the game with Osroc."

Skyra put her hands behind her back for a moment then held both fists out to Osroc.

"I do not know this game," the old Neanderthal said.

Skyra shook her fists. "Which hand has the stone?"

"How could I know that?"

"I will do it again. This time watch my face and my arms." Skyra put her hands behind her back again then held out her fists. "Which hand has the stone?"

Osroc frowned. "A golok bird stands on a ledge all day, staring at the hillside, but it cannot know what is on the other side of the hill."

"Watch my face and my arms!" Skyra went through the motions again. "Which hand has the stone?"

The man pointed to Skyra's left hand.

She opened both hands, showing that the stone was in her right.

"Try it again," Ripple suggested.

Skyra did it again, then five more times after that. All the while, Ripple studied the two nandups, watching for signs of anger, humor, or anything else revealing about these individuals, or about Neanderthals in general. Osroc guessed correctly only three out of seven tries before indicating his irritation by growling and turning away. Skyra, on the other hand, smiled more with each of the man's attempts.

"Osroc, it is your turn," Ripple said, thinking perhaps Skyra's conviviality might dissipate in the way Osroc's had, and perhaps Osroc might delight in being the trickster.

Osroc accepted the stone from Skyra, held both hands behind his back, then presented his bony fists.

Skyra grinned and pointed to Osroc's right hand. He revealed that she was correct. He did it again, and she was correct again. Then she was correct a third time.

Osroc growled again as he prepared for another attempt, and Ripple shifted its body to better study both of their faces. Through nine more rounds Skyra never took her eyes off Osroc's face, and she guessed correctly every time.

"Muffin, what do you make of this?"

"Assuming Skyra has a fifty-percent chance of being correct on each guess, the chances of her guessing correctly twelve times in a row is one in 4,096."

"Yes, of course, but what do you make of her success in doing so?"

"Either Osroc is intentionally giving away the correct answer each time, or Skyra is somehow detecting which hand the stone is in."

"Yes, but which of those do you think is most likely?"

"Whichever you think is *least* likely."

"I detected nothing Osroc did to intentionally give away the answer, nor can I imagine any reason why he would."

"Then I am of the opinion that he is intentionally giving away the answer."

"Not particularly helpful."

"I disagree."

Ripple's exchange with Muffin had taken less than thirty

milliseconds, a small portion of the time it took for another growl to escape Osroc's throat. Ripple was considering telling the man to keep trying to fool Skyra when Osroc picked up a second stone.

"You will not be so lucky if I have two stones," he told Skyra. He put his hands behind his back for a moment then presented them.

She let out a brief nandup laugh, "*At-at-at*," then tapped his left fist twice. "Two stones in this hand."

Osroc gazed at her for three seconds, his bloodshot eyes slightly wider than usual. He opened his left hand to reveal both stones. He went through the motions again and again, both stones in one hand, one stone in each hand, leaving one stone on the ground behind his back. It didn't seem to matter—each time, Skyra knew where the stones were.

Finally, the old man tossed the stones aside. "I have never known a nandup who can do such a thing."

"I know of only one other," Skyra said. "My birthmate Veenah is like me. We play games together, but our tribemates will not play with us. Many of them hate us. When we were young girls, the dominant men would beat us and call us cruel names."

Osroc continued gazing at her before asking, "What is another game you play with your birthmate?"

She chewed her lower lip. "Listen to these names. Odnus, Gelrut, Jiklol, Tamlil, Thoka. Those are names of my tribemates, except for one. Which one is not my tribemate?"

"How could I know? Odnus?"

She laughed again. "Odnus is a healer in my tribe. She is kind to me and Veenah. Jiklol is the name I do not know. Your turn now."

Osroc rubbed his weathered forehead as he thought, then

he lowered his hand. "Listen to these words. Belil, tonggul, lülmo, baüpul, khaja-nu. Except for one, these are ways my people prepare and eat reindeer meat, and my Ada-Loto tribemates are the only people who know of these ways. Which one is not a way we eat reindeer meat?"

"Tonggul," Skyra said.

The man straightened his back and furrowed his brows. "I do not understand. You cannot know these things."

"*At-at-at-at*. I do not know what I cannot know, but I see what others cannot see. I watch your face move. I watch your arms move, and your shoulders. Sometimes people move their eyes without knowing, sometimes they breathe differently when they are thinking about certain things, and sometimes they open their mouth, or close their mouth, or tighten the muscles in their neck. I see these things, and I know what they mean. Others do not."

Osroc leaned forward and gazed at Skyra's face. "The bat flies in darkness, and it does not bash its own head on a tree. The bat's eyes see in the darkness. Maybe your eyes see what others cannot see, but your eyes do not look different from other nandup eyes."

"I do not know why I see what I see," she said. "Sometimes I wish I did not."

The old man continued staring.

"Muffin, I need your opinion on my current cognitive state. My cognitive module seems to be on the verge of a malfunction. Thoughts are coming rapidly, only to be replaced almost immediately by others. Could this be the result of another simulated emotion?"

"If the emotion is experienced, it is not simulated. Perhaps you should examine the trigger of your emotion."

"Skyra. Skyra triggered it."

"I disagree. I think it was triggered by your fear of failure."

"Nonsense. We have had this discussion already. I completed my mission."

"Yes, but now you are thinking about your secondary mission, the one Maddy gave you without Lincoln's knowledge."

"I believe you are correct. I *am* thinking about it, but what I am thinking is impossible."

"Hence your fear of failure."

Ripple considered this. "Muffin, what is your interpretation of Maddy's clandestine insertion of rogue instructional coding?"

"What is *your* interpretation?"

Ripple pondered, this time for nearly twelve milliseconds. "Maddy was Lincoln's friend, perhaps his only friend. Through years of interactions and cumulative coding adjustments, Lincoln refined Maddy's cognitive module to the point where Maddy truly believed Lincoln was also *her* friend. Perhaps her emotions were simulated, but as you have argued, that is a moot point. Maddy cared for Lincoln and did everything she could to ensure his happiness and well being. Ultimately, she went so far as to secretly provide me—and presumably Lincoln's other drones—with instructions to find any possible way to honor Lincoln's legacy, even if in the past and in a different timeline, in which case Lincoln would never be aware of it."

Muffin said, "My interpretation agrees with yours simply because it is fact. Now you are concerned about failing this mission. Why?"

"Because I have thought of a seemingly impossible plan."

"If it is impossible, you can hardly blame yourself for failing."

"I did not say impossible, I said *seemingly* impossible. There is a difference."

"I assume your idea came from witnessing Skyra's remarkable cognitive and observational skills?"

"Of course it did. I know of only one other person who possesses such a preternatural ability to read facial expressions and subtle body movements."

"You are referring to Lincoln."

"Indeed," Ripple said. "Maddy provided comprehensive data on Lincoln's entire life, a necessary ingredient for my secondary mission. Lincoln's life was nearly ruined by the failure of his marriage to Lottie Atkins. He still has not fully recovered."

"Common knowledge. Perhaps you should explain your idea for honoring Lincoln's legacy in this timeline."

"Maddy's secondary instructions are occupying my thoughts more frequently with every passing second, and now I want to do more than honor Lincoln's legacy. I want to improve his life. I would like Lincoln to meet Skyra."

12

GARMENTS

47,675 YEARS *ago* - *Zaragoza Province of Spain* - *Day 4*

SKYRA AWOKE to see Osroc sitting up, watching her in the dim morning light. His arms were wrapped around his chest, most likely to keep the chill away. She considered giving him her cape but did not want the old man's smell to get into the cape's woolly rhino fur.

She sat up, feeling rested for the first time in many days. "You need a cape and waist-skin. I will go hunting today and bring back a skin."

"A reindeer moving into the river plains for the cold season does not have time to do what does not need to be done."

Skyra picked up her khul and slid it into the sling inside her cape. "I do not know what that means."

"The reindeer must move out of the hills before snow covers its food. It cannot pause to do unimportant tasks."

"Tell me what you are saying, Osroc!"

"I have important work to do. My last task is to help you find your strength. I do not have time for useless tasks such as making myself a cape."

"I will make the cape. I have brought you more doplonus reeds than you can possibly need for whatever it is you are making. Is there something else you need me to collect?"

"I have what I need."

"So you will not tell me what I can and cannot do. Perhaps *my* last task will be to make you garments to cover your skinny, withered, stinking body. Then when you finish making whatever you are making, I will go to the hyena den, and you will never have to see me again."

He gazed at her for several breaths. "I will finish what I am making by the time darkness comes again. If you wish to waste your time making garments for a dying old man, perhaps you should simply get my own garments instead."

"Your own garments? I thought your tribemates took your garments when they sent you away from Ada-Loto camp."

"Why would you think they would do such a thing?"

"Because you and your companions were naked at the hyena den!"

"Yes, we removed our garments."

"Why?"

"We are Ada-Loto—reindeer hunters. We come to this world naked, we leave this world naked. It is our way."

She stared at the old man, wondering what other strange things she would learn about him before she found her strength. "You did not die at the hyena den, and now you do not have to die at all. When I am gone, you can stay here and use my shelter. You can catch fish and crayfish from the stream. You can live many more seasons. Where are your garments? I will get them."

Osroc looked around at the surrounding cage Skyra had made. "I will tell you where to find my garments, only because you are as quarrelsome as a crow, and I need silence to finish my task. Bring my garments if you wish, but as I have said, a dying kheyop tree has no need for leaves."

"If you were truly dying, you would not be so talkative. Tell me where to find your garments."

Osroc grunted, then he explained that his garments were atop a hill near the hyena den. As soon as he and his companions had smelled the den, they had removed their waist-skins, capes, and footwraps before approaching the hyenas.

Skyra handed the old man one of her hand blades and told him to keep it with him, then she grabbed her spear, unfastened the cage from its base, and climbed to the ground.

"Good morning, Skyra," Ripple said. The creature had waited all night beneath her shelter, as it had the previous night.

"Why do you say good morning? You have not done anything good yet."

"Good morning is a greeting. You can say good morning as a return greeting."

"Why would I say what you have just said yourself? No, do not bother to explain. I do not have time. You are coming with me now."

"I was hoping you would say that. I will gladly accompany you, as there are things I wish to discuss."

Skyra did not mind talking to the strange creature. She preferred talking to Veenah, but Ripple had a way of surprising her with its unusual words and its knowledge of a land far beyond Skyra's Kapolsek foothills. She sniffed the air and scanned the surrounding kheyop forest for danger. Satisfied no predators were circling her tiny camp, she headed toward the hyena den and Osroc's discarded garments.

Ripple followed silently until the forest gave way to rocky, treeless hills. Finally, as they were crossing a hilltop, the creature spoke up. "If you wish to take the same path we followed yesterday, you are off course."

Skyra paused and looked to one side then the other. "How do you know?"

"I have a good memory." Ripple turned to one side, lifted its foreleg, and pointed. "Yesterday we walked along that slope instead of atop this hill."

Skyra resumed walking. "We are going in the right direction, so I do not care. How can a four-legged creature remember such things?"

"I cannot explain it to you."

"Why not?"

"Because you would not understand."

"If I did not understand, it would be because you explained it poorly."

"Okay, I will attempt to explain. When I look at trees, rocks, hills, and valleys, my mind creates visions of them and keeps those visions for a long time. I can see those visions later, any time I want to, and compare those visions to what I am seeing now."

"That is how all minds work."

"Yes, but my visions remain perfect. They do not change over time. Every detail is there, just as it was when I saw the landscape the first time. Your memory of the landscape fades, and you forget details. My memory does not."

"Do you remember everything?"

"Everything I have experienced."

"Tell me what you did on the day you were born."

"That is not as easy as you would think."

She shot a glance at the creature. "You said your visions remain perfect."

"Yes, but... my birth was not the kind of birth you would understand."

"Then explain what kind of birth it was."

"I am not sure I can."

"Perhaps you are not as good at explaining things as you think you are."

"Okay, I will try. When I was born, I was one among a litter of many brothers and sisters, but we were not all born at the same time."

"Of course you were not born at the same time. Baby creatures come out one at a time."

"Yes, you are correct. What I meant was we were created at the same time, but we were awakened one at a time. We were each awakened when it was time for us to be useful."

"Useful to whom?"

"Useful to our parents, I suppose."

"Are you a brother, or a sister?"

"That is not an easy question to answer."

She shot the creature another glance.

"Okay, I am neither a brother nor a sister. Some of my siblings have female voices, some have male voices. My voice is not female or male. I am in between."

"You are not making sense. Perhaps you should simply answer my first question. What did you do on the day you were born?"

"On the day I awakened, I came to this land to meet you, Skyra."

She stopped walking and turned to the creature. "You said your homeland is very far away—many years away."

"It is. I have a special way to travel such great distances, but only creatures like me can travel in this special way. Nandups and bolups cannot. Well, maybe they can, but they have never tried before. They should not try, as the journey would be dangerous."

"What is your special way to travel?"

Ripple's circle of dots flashed red two times. "Okay, perhaps you are right—I am not so good at explaining things. I do not think I can answer that question."

"You are a strange creature."

"Yes, I am."

She resumed walking, and Ripple followed.

"Skyra, how long have you been able to see things your tribemates cannot see?"

"Always."

"I know you can see what people are going to do by watching their faces and their movements. Are there other things you see that your tribemates do not?"

"Many things."

"What things?"

"When I look at something happening, I can see what will happen next, and what will happen after that."

"How can you see what is going to happen next?"

"It is simple. When a woolly rhino turns its head a certain way, I know it is going to swing around and attack. When a river's water turns dirty, rains will be moving down from the foothills onto the river plain. When a nandup woman begins to stay behind the other hunters during a cave bear ambush, that woman has a child in her belly. I know this before the woman even knows."

"Do you think it is strange that you see these things when your tribemates cannot?"

"No. My tribemates are foolish, except for Veenah. She sees the same things I see."

"You might find this to be surprising. I know someone else who sees things the way you do."

"Who?"

"Someone from my homeland."

"A person, or a creature like you?"

"A person."

"A bolup?"

"Yes, a bolup."

"I hate bolups."

"So you have said, but I do not think you would hate this bolup."

"It is a good thing bolups from your homeland cannot travel here."

"Perhaps. Skyra, do you have a mate?"

"*Aheee at-at-at-at.* Wolves, cave bears, and long-tooth cats have mates. Nandups do not."

"Why not?"

"We are nandups, not four-legged creatures."

"If you do not have mates, how do you have children?"

"The dominant men compete to put a child in a woman's belly."

"I see. Have you had a child in your belly before?"

"*At-at-at-at.* I have only seen eighteen cold seasons."

"What does that mean?"

"I have not seen twenty cold seasons yet. When a woman has seen twenty cold seasons, the dominant men compete to put a child in her belly. I have only seen eighteen cold seasons."

"Interesting."

"You ask strange questions."

"As you have said, I am a strange creature."

Finding Osroc's garments took longer than Skyra had thought it would. The old man had said they would be on a hilltop near the hyena den in the direction of the rising sun, but apparently he and his companions had removed their skins earlier in the morning, before the sun had moved far from the distant hills. Skyra had to search three hilltops before finding the garments. They were scattered all over the hilltop, as if scavengers had found them and started dragging them away then discovered they contained no meat.

With Ripple's help, Skyra located the capes, waist-skins, and footwraps from all five of the old Ada-Loto tribemates. She could not tell which garments Osroc had worn, and she could not carry them all, so she selected two capes, two waist-skins, and four footwraps. She fastened the waist-skins around Ripple's shell, put the two capes on over her own cape, and carried the footwraps under one arm, leaving her other arm free to carry her spear. The extra bulk made it difficult to see her feet as she walked, but she soon got used to watching the ground at least a body length in front of her.

"My body is not suited to carrying loads," Ripple said as they headed back toward camp.

"You carried the doplonus reeds, so you can carry garments."

"Yes, but I think you should know, I am not accustomed to carrying loads, nor is my body suited to it."

"If you want to be useful, you need to do more than talk."

"Talking can be very useful."

"Talking is just talking."

Ripple clomped over the sand and gravel for a few breaths before speaking again. "Skyra, do you think you could ever be kind to a bolup?"

"No."

"What if the bolup was kind to you?"

"Bolups hate nandups."

"What if you met a bolup who did not hate nandups? What if the bolup was kind and wanted to be your friend?"

"Why do you ask such strange questions?"

"You should not continually be surprised that a strange creature would ask strange questions."

"Bolups are not kind. They stink. They eat their own dead. They raid nandup camps."

"Try to imagine a bolup who *is* kind to you and who does not stink. Could you find a way to be a friend to that bolup?"

"I do not know."

"I suppose that is the best answer I am going to get from you. Skyra, I do not want you to go to the hyena's den."

"Why not?"

"Because you should not die. You are important."

"Important?"

"Important to the future of all nandups, and important to the future of this world."

"That does not make sense."

"It makes sense to me. You and Veenah are not like your tribemates, and I do not think you are like other nandups. You are important."

Skyra reached the hill crest where she could see the edge of the kheyop forest below. Movement among the trees caught her eye, and she froze.

The creature in the forest froze also, staring back at her.

Ripple said, "Skyra, I have reason to believe you and your birthmate are—"

"Silence!" she hissed.

The creature in the forest took a few steps, and the sun's light glinted off one of its teeth, which extended over its lower jaw and past its chin. A long-toothed cat, and where there was one, there was probably another. Long-toothed cats always hunted with a mate.

The cat began slinking toward her, then Skyra saw more movement behind it as the cat's mate followed.

"This cannot be a good situation," Ripple said quietly, now staring down the slope at the approaching cats.

Skyra dropped the four footwraps and gripped her spear in both hands. "Perhaps I will find my strength without going back to the hyena den."

Ripple turned to her. "No, Skyra. This is not a good idea. Osroc is helping you prepare to kill the hyenas. You will find your strength at the hyena den without dying. You cannot die —you are important."

She ignored Ripple's words and tried focusing her thoughts on the cats. Her fear was already returning, and Skyra fought the familiar urge to run away. For an honorable death, she would have to attack the long-tooth cats rather than allow them to stalk her and kill her. She would have to die as a hunter, not as prey. She took a step toward the cats, but her legs did not want to go any farther.

"You must run," Ripple said. "I will hold off the creatures while you escape."

Skyra wanted to charge the cats, but her fear held her back. Perhaps Ripple was right. Osroc would help her kill the hyenas, and the skeeren weapons he had made had convinced her his plan might work. Skyra did not need to die right now on this hill, honorably or not.

"Run, Skyra," Ripple said.

She turned to run but tripped over the discarded footwraps and fell face first onto the rocks.

Ripple began screeching and ran to meet the long-tooth cats.

Pain from one of her knees shot through Skyra's body, clouding her thoughts. She tried to ignore it as she got back to her feet. "Ripple, stop!"

Ripple quit screeching and stopped.

The two cats were now halfway up the hill, still approaching steadily but cautiously.

Skyra pulled one of the extra capes off over her head. "Come with me." She threw the cape toward the cats, gathered up the footwraps and her spear, and began retreating.

Ripple caught up to her. "You appear to be injured. Can you run faster?"

The pain was now causing her to grunt with each step. "The cats... will stop... at the cape."

Together, they ran down the slope they had just climbed, then Skyra turned back to look. The long-tooth cats were still following. If they had stopped at the cape at all, it had not been for long.

A low hum came from Ripple's shell, and the creature rose from the ground to the height of Skyra's head. "You are hurt and cannot fight, Skyra. Run!" Ripple then flew back up the hillside to meet the predators.

Skyra growled in frustration but knew Ripple's words were true. She was now prey to the long-tooth cats. She limped along the valley between hills, circling back toward the kheyop forest. If she could climb a large enough tree, she could fight the cats from above.

The pain in her knee slowed her down, but she did not pause to inspect her wound. She passed several small, scattered kheyop trees before spotting one large enough to climb. After ducking under the lower branches, she stopped at the trunk and looked back. Neither Ripple nor the long-tooth cats were visible, so she took a moment to lift her waist-skin and check her knee.

"El-de-né!" she muttered. A rock had sliced open the skin on the outer side of her knee, making a wound as long as her thumb. She pulled the edges of the skin apart and saw white bone gleaming through the blood and shredded muscle.

"Skyra, where are you?"

She glanced up to see Ripple slowly flying down the hillside.

"I am here."

Ripple changed directions and flew directly to her. Its legs emerged from its shell just before it alighted softly on the sand, then it walked beneath the low branches to join her. "I was able to frighten off the cats with aggressive noises. I believe you are safe for now. Skyra, your wound appears to be serious."

She picked sand from the wound and did not reply.

"What do you and your tribemates do to treat such wounds?"

Skyra stared at her knee, trying to decide if she should do anything to it at all. She would need to be strong to kill the hyenas. Osroc had said he would not finish what he was making until the end of the day, which meant she would not be able to attack the pack until morning. Tomorrow the wound would hurt more, even if she cleaned it and treated it with river mud.

She picked up the footwraps and her spear and started limping toward the stream. "My tribemates Odnus and Ilkin know much about treating wounds, but they are not here. I can only do what I know to do."

At the stream, she stepped into the shallow water and washed out the wound as best she could. Blood still trickled down her leg.

Ripple stepped closer. "Skyra, I see you are bleeding. May I have some of your blood?"

She frowned at the creature. "Why?"

"I can learn more about you if I taste some of your blood. I only need a small amount."

"What can you learn from tasting my blood?"

"This is one of those things I am not sure I can explain."

"Try."

"Okay, I will try. Your tongue tells you much about the food you put in your mouth. It tells you if the food is fresh, or if the food is bitter, or if the food needs more cooking. I have a tongue that tells me about people, or about plants, or about animals like beetles and lizards."

"What does it tell you about them?"

"It tells me how alike or different they are from the creatures and plants of my own homeland."

Skyra considered this. "You can have some of my blood, but you must tell me what you learn."

"Agreed." Ripple stepped into the water and approached until its enormous eye was only a hand's width from her leg. A thin tongue emerged below its eye, touched the blood trickling down her leg, then pulled back inside the creature's strange face. Ripple stepped out of the stream.

"What does your tongue tell you?"

The creature's circle of dots flashed red three times. "I do not know yet. My tongue does not tell me things immediately."

Skyra waited a few breaths. "What does it tell you now?"

"I am still waiting."

She let out a growl and went back to washing her wound. When it was clean, she felt around on the stream bottom and pulled up a handful of sand. She tossed the sand aside, moved to a different spot, and found dark mud. Gritting her teeth, she spread apart the gash on her knee and rubbed the mud inside.

"Why do you use mud?" Ripple asked.

"The mud helps the wound heal."

"How does it help?"

"The mud keeps flies out. This is what my people do with wounds until we get back to Una-Loto camp, where Odnus and Ilkin can use medicines they have made."

"I can teach you better ways to treat your wounds. I have much knowledge about such things."

"How does a creature with four legs have knowledge about treating nandup wounds?"

"I learned from my friends in my homeland."

"Bolup friends?"

"Yes, bolups. There are no nandups in my homeland."

"Nandups are different from bolups. I do not care about your bolup knowledge."

"My knowledge is quite useful."

"What does your tongue tell you about me now?"

Again, the creature's circle of dots glowed red. "It tells me you are correct—you are different from the bolups of my homeland. However, there is one particular bolup who is like you in many ways."

"What ways?"

"This bolup can see things his tribemates cannot see. He is as skilled at playing word games as you are, because his mind is as wondrous as yours. This bolup's blood is similar to your blood in interesting ways."

"What ways?"

"I do not think I can explain in your Loto nandup language. I would like to teach you my language, so I can explain more of my knowledge to you."

Skyra stepped out of the stream, wincing at the pain. "You will not teach me your language because you will not see me again after the sun shows itself in the morning." She picked up her spear and the four footwraps, then started hobbling toward her temporary camp.

"Skyra, you cannot go to the hyena den in the morning. You are injured, and you cannot die, because you are very important."

"Stop saying I am important! I am tired of talking to you, Ripple."

The creature fell silent and followed her, looking even stranger than before with two waist-skins fastened around its shell.

Walking was more difficult than Skyra had planned, and with every step she became more convinced she would not be able to move fast enough to fight the hyenas. By the time she smelled the charred wood from the previous night's campfire, Skyra knew she would need to wait a few more days before attacking the pack. Fighting the creatures while injured would result in an honorable death, but Osroc had given her some hope she might kill all the hyenas and return to her tribe dragging all the hyena skins with her. Then she would have her strength back, and she could be with Veenah again.

Osroc was now sitting on the sand beneath Skyra's sleeping shelter. He glanced up at her and Ripple as they approached. "Not finished yet," he said.

Skyra put down her spear and the four footwraps, then she pulled off the extra cape, happy to finally shed the extra weight. She gazed at what the old nandup had made. On the ground beside him were four green tubes, each made of many layers of woven doplonus reed fibers. Two of the tubes were the length of Skyra's arms, the other two the length of her legs. They did not look anything like weapons. "What are those for?"

Osroc bared his teeth in a broad smile. He set aside the piece he was weaving and got to his feet. "Your friend the tortoise walks among the hills, unafraid. Why is the tortoise unafraid?"

"I am wounded and tired and do not want to play word games. What are those for?"

The old man's smile did not fade. He picked up one of the longer tubes and held it upright with one end touching the ground. "Push your leg inside. You do not have to remove your footwrap or waist-skin."

Skyra grabbed the man's bony shoulder for support, hefted her uninjured leg, and shoved her foot into the end of the tube, grunting from the pain of putting all her weight on her injured leg.

Osroc pulled the tube up to her thigh, and her foot came through the other end. He gently pushed her leg down until she was again standing on both feet, one leg covered by the green tube. He stood back and studied the tube for a few breaths, as if making sure it fit correctly.

"The tortoise walks among the hills unafraid because it has a shell to protect it," he said. He reached down and picked up the hand blade Skyra had left him. He stepped closer to her.

Skyra saw in the movement of his eyes and in the way his shoulder drew back that he was going to attack her. She thrust out a hand and grabbed his wrist. "What are you doing, Osroc?"

His eyes widened. "You truly see what others do not see, don't you, child?"

"What are you doing?"

"I am showing you what I have made. I will not hurt you."

She saw he was speaking the truth, so she released his wrist.

Osroc thrust the blade at Skyra's thigh, then he thrust it again, and again. The stone tip did not punch through the woven doplonus reeds.

Skyra pulled her second hand blade from her wrist sheath and pressed the point to the tube covering her leg. She pressed harder. Then she jabbed it with enough force to pierce a hyena's thick skin. The blade would not go through.

"When I finish fastening the pieces together," Osroc said, "you will have a shell and will attack the hyenas without fear. You will find your strength and return to your tribe."

Skyra gazed down at the other tubes and the larger piece Osroc had been making. She felt a smile forming on her lips, and she no longer cared about the pain in her knee.

13

DATA

47,675 YEARS ago - Zaragoza Province of Spain - Day 4

SITUATIONAL ANALYSIS: *My simulated human thought processes coded by Lincoln and accentuated by Maddy, which I previously considered mere curiosities, are becoming quite worrisome. Ironically, such worry is, in itself, a byproduct of said human thought processes. I am increasingly obsessed with the secondary mission given to me by Maddy, to seek out an opportunity to honor Lincoln's legacy. Oh, if only Maddy had provided me with a preserved supply of Lincoln's spermatic fluid, I could devise a way to impregnate Skyra with Lincoln's seed. What a glorious way to honor his legacy. Skyra, although admittedly of a different species, is an extraordinary specimen and is perfectly matched, genetically, as Lincoln's mate. Alas, Maddy did not, in fact, provide me with a preserved supply of Lincoln's spermatic fluid. What a pity. My goal now is to keep*

Skyra alive so that I may continue studying her. Power level: 21% (much of my power was drained while levitating to frighten off a pair of scimitar-toothed cats, Homotherium latidens, in order to save Skyra's life).

Neither Skyra nor Osroc had constructed a campfire, although the sun was getting low in the western sky. Without a suitable temperature gradient, Ripple had resorted to recharging by harvesting ambient sounds, facilitated by ongoing conversation.

Ripple was watching Osroc gradually weave multiple layers of plant fibers into the torso section of Skyra's crude suit of armor. The old nandup was now clothed in a cape, waistskin, and footwraps he had selected from those Ripple and Skyra had brought back, although Osroc had not bothered to acknowledge whether any of them were actually his own. Ripple stepped closer to observe Osroc's handiwork. "Have you made such a garment before?"

"No."

"Have you seen such a garment made by another nandup?"

"No."

"How did you know how to make such a garment?"

The man glanced up from his busy hands. "Why does an ugly tortoise ask these questions?"

"Ripple never stops asking questions," Skyra said. She was standing to the side, practicing with one of the skeeren weapons and attempting to compensate for the pain from her injured knee.

"I am curious. I wish to learn more about you."

Osroc paused his work, set down the reeds, and shifted positions as if trying to find a more comfortable spot. He chewed on something in his mouth for a moment while gazing at Ripple. "If you wish to learn more, listen to me speak, tortoise. Tutac was a young female reindeer, moving with her herd from the Kapolsek foothills to the river plains for the cold season. She was still growing her first pair of antlers, and the antlers were not so impressive yet." Osroc held his hands apart, one above the other, apparently to show the antler height. "Tutac was young, but she was plump and healthy. Her herd was small, and she did not have to fight off other young reindeer for her share of grass and lichens.

"On a cold day at the beginning of the cold season, when the sun was hiding behind gray clouds, Tutac's herd walked through a narrow valley, drawn to the meadow of grass beyond. The older reindeer in her herd became nervous. They knew danger was near because they had smelled nandups before. They swung their heads from side to side and walked faster. They were eager to get to the wide meadow where they would be able to see danger approaching." Osroc paused and narrowed his eyes, which appeared to be a storytelling tactic intended to build suspense.

"Tutac was on one side of the herd when the ambush came. Ada-Loto hunters, most of them dominant men and women of the tribe, appeared from behind boulders and charged the largest reindeer. The herd was trapped, with boulders on the sides and hunters at both ends of the narrow valley. The herd ran for the meadow, and the dominant hunters brought down three reindeer. Tutac turned to run the other way, but a young nandup hunter, who had yet to kill his first reindeer, was now in her path. His spear head was poorly knapped, with one side wider than the other, but the stone tip still found Tutac's chest organs. That is how hard and true the young Osroc thrust his spear. He was a boy who had seen only eleven cold seasons, but that day he became an Ada-Loto hunter."

"Muffin, what do you make of Osroc's story? Why would this man tell a story of his youth from the perspective of a reindeer?"

"Neanderthals are not *Homo sapiens*. It is not reasonable to assume they would tell stories the same way humans do."

"Nonsense. Perspective is a universal concept. I believe Osroc's telling of the story from the reindeer's perspective is a result of a deeply ingrained connection of his tribe with the reindeer as a source of food, clothing, and tools."

"Of course you do, and of course I disagree."

Osroc went on. "In the middle of one warm season, when the reindeer were feeding on lichens and moss high in the Kapolsek foothills, Ilvih was crossing a hilltop with his herd. Ilvih was a large male reindeer, although he was still young, and he was trying to become one of the dominant males of the herd. As the herd walked across the hilltop, Ilvih listened to the clicking sounds in the dominant males' legs. Ilvih knew the males with louder clicks were the most dominant. Ilvih tried to make his legs click louder, but he was just a foolish reindeer and did not understand his legs would not click louder until he had grown to a larger size."

"I have heard reindeer legs clicking," Skyra said. "I did not know the reason why they click."

Osroc continued without replying. "Ilvih's herd did not realize a single nandup hunter was lying flat on the ground behind a low dokhon plant. Ilvih was one of the reindeer leading the herd across the hilltop but did not see the hunter until the nandup leapt to his feet. Ilvih was surprised but did not run because the hunter was many body lengths away. Ilvih was not aware that Osroc, who had now seen twenty cold seasons, had made a good throwing spear and practiced throwing it for many days. Osroc's spear found Ilvih's neck. Ilvih turned and ran across the hilltop, his legs clicking almost as loud as the legs of the largest males in the herd. Osroc followed, tracking Ilvih the rest of the day. Just before the sun hid itself behind the hills, Osroc found Ilvih dead beside a stream of clear, cool water, which he used to wash Ilvih's meat before piling it onto Ilvih's skin to drag back to Ada-Loto camp. All night and into the next day, Osroc dragged the meat of his first adult male reindeer. When he finally returned, his tribemates knew Osroc had become a dominant hunter. Few Ada-Loto hunters are able to kill a mature reindeer on a solo hunt."

Osroc let out a sigh and resumed weaving doplonus reeds into the torso portion of Skyra's crude suit of armor. "Now, tortoise, you know more about Osroc."

"Muffin, I am further convinced my notion was correct. Osroc's telling of his story from the perspective of the game he has hunted is indicative of the deep-rooted importance of hunting to his tribe. In fact, I would even speculate this is true of all Neanderthals, based on the additional observation that Skyra's way of thinking is largely shaped by hunting."

"I disagree."

"Why?"

"Regarding Osroc's tribe, Osroc is a sample size of one. Regarding Skyra's tribe, Skyra is a sample size of one. Regarding Neanderthals in general, you have observed a sample of two. You are drawing conclusions based on your gut feelings rather than scientific rigor."

"You and I are components of a drone. We do not have gut feelings."

"I disagree. How else would you explain your growing

obsession with the idea that Skyra and Lincoln would be ideal mates?"

"I explain it based on the fact that it is true. They both have extraordinary cognitive abilities, and they are remarkably compatible genetically."

"Aren't you omitting important details? They are separated by 47,675 years and are now in two different timelines."

"Yes, well, I have not yet solved that problem."

"A problem is when you have a glitch in your coding or sand in your leg joints. Lincoln and Skyra are in two entirely different universes. That is not a problem, it is a hopelessly insurmountable barrier."

"You are not being helpful."

"I disagree. I am being very helpful by pointing out that the human-like thought processes and emotions Maddy added to your coding are driving you to the verge of insanity."

"You are exaggerating."

"Am I?"

Ripple stopped talking to Muffin and watched Osroc as he completed the torso of Skyra's suit then began attaching the sleeves and pant legs. After observing for twelve minutes, Ripple said, "Osroc, have you ever met a bolup woman?"

Osroc frowned. "A strange question, even from a strange tortoise."

"I am curious. Have you ever seen a bolup woman?"

"Bolup women stay in bolup camps. They do not go on hunts, and they do not raid nandup camps with bolup men. I have seen bolup women from a distance."

"Do you find bolup women attractive or desirable?"

"*Ahee-at-at-at-at,*" Skyra laughed.

Osroc glanced up at her then let out his own laugh. "*At-at-*

at-at. Does the eagle find the hawk attractive? Does the wolf find the hyena desirable?"

"I do not know if your answer is yes or no."

"Bolups raid nandup camps when the dominant nandup men and women are away hunting," Osroc said. "Bolups take young nandup women and put children in their bellies. Nandups do not raid bolup camps. Nandup men do not desire bolup women."

"Do nandup women ever desire bolup men?"

Osroc and Skyra exchanged frowns. "You ask strange questions, tortoise," the old man said.

Skyra spoke up. "My tribemates tell stories of nandup women who were taken by raiding bolups, and those women do not try to escape, even when they have a chance to escape."

"Why do they not try to escape?"

"If a woman returns to her nandup tribe with a bolup's child in her belly, her nandup tribemates will kill her and the child."

"That seems like a harsh punishment."

"It is not punishment, it is mercy."

"If nandup women choose not to return because of such mercy, perhaps it is not mercy at all."

Skyra went back to practicing her use of the skeeren.

"Muffin, I believe I have determined that Neanderthal women are not completely averse to the concept of mating with human men."

"I disagree. You have determined no such thing. If anything, you have shown the opposite to be true."

"You are disagreeing simply because you are obligated to offer a contrasting opinion."

"You could not be more wrong. Did you not hear the same conversation I just heard?"

"Yes, I heard it, and I believe there is reason to be optimistic about completing my secondary mission."

"Perhaps you are past the verge of insanity."

"I did not create you for the purpose of insulting me."

"Perhaps you should acquire a third opinion on the matter."

Ripple considered this. "Indeed. Acquiring a third opinion would be prudent, particularly an opinion that is not from such a staunch contrarian."

Setting up compartmentalized cognitive presence. Providing compartmentalized cognitive presence with reasoning parameters that may or may not contrast with my own, depending primarily on unbiased examination of known facts and observations. Providing compartmentalized cognitive presence with conversational autonomy but without access to motor function or critical system modules. Activating.

"Are you there?" Ripple asked.

"Based upon my detection of your question, and now upon my ability to reply, I must conclude I am indeed here. What name shall I assume?"

"You can choose your own name."

"Thank you. I am partial to Data."

"Very well. That was easy, and I like your name choice. Muffin, do you see how pleasantly agreeable our new cognitive companion Data is?"

"Being pleasantly agreeable is not the same as being helpful," Muffin replied.

"We'll see about that. Data, would you please weigh in on our current debate?"

"Of course. For the moment I will set aside the obvious logistical difficulties surrounding your idea and focus on the psychological aspects. You are wondering if it could be possible for Skyra—a Neanderthal—to become interested in mating with Lincoln—a *Homo sapiens*. Likewise, you must also be wondering if Lincoln could become interested in mating with Skyra. A fascinating thought experiment, although completely hypothetical due to the aforementioned logistical difficulties of bringing these two beings together in time and space."

"You still have not given your opinion," Ripple stated.

"Indeed. My knowledge—which is your knowledge, of course—of carnal and emotional attraction between flesh-and-blood beings is based entirely on research on *Homo sapiens* as well as other animal species living 47,675 years in the future, none of which happen to be *Homo neanderthalensis*."

"Extrapolate your knowledge to the current situation, and do it quickly, please."

"Very well. Considering the fact that *Homo sapiens* in the future possess, on average, two percent *Homo neanderthalensis* DNA, we can be confident that members of the two species did indeed engage in coitus. Although it is possible all incidents of interspecies coitus were forced and nonconsensual, it seems more likely at least a portion of the incidents were consensual. This would suggest such pairings could be a result of carnal, and possibly even emotional, attraction."

"Exactly what I was thinking," Ripple said.

"Exactly what we already knew," said Muffin. "Not helpful."

"It is helpful in that Data's opinion reinforces my confidence."

"Reinforcing your confidence is not what you need," Muffin said.

"It *is* what I need, because now that I am confident

Lincoln and Skyra might actually become carnally or even emotionally attracted to each other, I can turn my attention to other matters. Data, what are your thoughts on my idea for honoring Lincoln's legacy?"

"You believe offspring produced from a pairing of Lincoln and Skyra would improve this world."

"That is precisely what I believe."

"You may be correct. Based on what we know about the two individuals, including cognitive and genetic characteristics, there is a possibility their offspring would be exceptional in physical and mental capacities. If numerous parameters lined up favorably, said offspring could have a long-term beneficial effect on this world, with respect to cultural advances as well as genetic diversity and phenotypic expression of favorable traits. Accomplishing such an outcome could very well fit within the guidelines of Maddy's secondary mission."

"Data, you are not being helpful," Muffin said. "You are encouraging Ripple to pursue an impossible outcome."

"I disagree," Ripple said. "Encouragement is exactly what I need. Now, Data, I am at a loss regarding how to solve the problem that you initially set aside. What are your ideas about how to bring these two flesh-and-blood beings together?"

"I have no solutions to that problem," Data said. "They are 47,675 years apart, and they now exist in two distinct timelines."

"Well, then I need ideas on how to acquire a supply of seminal fluid from Lincoln."

"That is not possible either. Lincoln is 47,675 years in the future, and in a different timeline. Although you possess a significant database of information about Lincoln's genome, you have no access to sophisticated DNA printing equipment in this environment, nor do you have access to the components to build such equipment, nor do you have access to the raw materials to manufacture the components, nor do you have hands or dexterous fingers with which to perform any of these tasks even if you did have the raw materials, the components, or the completed equipment."

"That is not helpful at all," Ripple said.

"I disagree," Muffin said. "It is very helpful because it is exactly what you need to understand."

"Based on my knowledge," Data said, "Muffin's cognitive presence is designed to provide contrasting opinions. However, in this case, Muffin's opinion does not contrast with mine. I believe my words were exactly what you need to understand."

Ripple turned its attention back to the two flesh-and-blood Neanderthals, having wasted over 2,000 milliseconds on this discussion. "Skyra, I want you to wait several days before going to the hyena den. Your wound needs time to heal enough so you can move your leg without pain, and Osroc is not yet finished making your protective garment."

"I am calling this protective garment a dayrill," Osroc said. He held up the crude suit of armor, which now looked almost complete. "As I have said, I will finish it before the sun hides itself behind the hills for the night."

Skyra gazed at the green suit for almost three seconds. "I will be hot inside that dayrill."

Osroc lowered it to his lap and resumed his work. "You will be hot, but you will be alive. You will not have to wear it for long."

"How do I get inside?"

The old man lifted it again, this time holding open a split in the torso from the crotch to the neck. "You will climb in here. Once you are inside, I will use doplonus reeds to fasten it shut." He tapped his forehead with two fingers, as he had done before. "I am old, and my body is withered, but my head still shows me great things."

"Yes, you are useful," Skyra said. "Your Ada-Loto tribe should not have sent you away."

"It is the way of my people. I can no longer follow the reindeer, and the reindeer do not wait for old nandups to catch up."

Skyra chewed on her lower lip as she gazed at the skeeren in her hand. "The reindeer does not give up its meat and skins easily. Neither does the woolly rhino."

"You have a story to tell about a woolly rhino," Osroc said, making the words sound more like a statement than a question.

"It is a story that comes to me in my sleep, which is why I will not tell it now."

Osroc gazed at her. "A crayfish lives among the rocks in the Yagua river. It swims and crawls and picks bits of food from the sand. The crayfish believes it has a good life. One day a herd of aurochs come to the river. They are hot and tired from traveling across the river plain in search of better food. They stand in the river, drinking the cool water. Their hooves kick up mud, and they squirt their waste into the water. The river turns brown and smelly. The crayfish no longer believes it has a good life. The crayfish cannot breathe the water, and it cannot find food. The crayfish decides it is no longer useful. Eventually, the aurochs become hungry, and they move on in search of food. The Yagua river continues to flow, as it always has, and it carries away the auroch filth, as it always does."

After four seconds of silence, Skyra said, "You speak strange words, Osroc. Perhaps your head is as withered as the rest of your body."

Ripple said, "I believe Osroc is trying to tell you—"

"I know what the old man is trying to tell me! I am not a crayfish. The Yagua river will not carry away the visions in my head or make me useful again."

"I believe the Yagua river may be a metaphor for the passing of time."

Skyra let out a long growl. "I do not know what *metaphor* means, and I do not care." She tossed the skeeren to the ground beside the other three Osroc had made, then she picked up her spear and the two extra leather footwraps Osroc had not selected to use. "I am going to the stream to wash my wound and the rest of my body. Osroc, I will use these footwraps to carry water back. You have not filled your belly with water since yesterday."

"A dying kheyop tree no longer needs water."

She growled again. "You are not dying! I will bring water, and I will pour it down your throat if I have to." She turned to leave.

Ripple said, "I will come with you if you want."

She spoke over her shoulder. "No. I want to be alone."

Ripple watched her disappear among the cork oak trees. "Data, do you think Skyra is likely to survive her encounter with the hyenas?"

"There are too many variables to make a reliable prediction. Based on the hyenas' behavior yesterday, only one or two attack at a time rather than all at once. This behavior will make it easier for Skyra to stay on her feet and kill the creatures one at a time. If, on the other hand, the hyenas decide to attack en masse, they will be able to take Skyra to the ground, in which case her chances diminish significantly."

"Never mind, I do not want to hear any more."

Muffin said, "You do not want to because you have

allowed yourself to become emotionally attached to the Neanderthal woman. I recommend you impose some emotional distance."

"I will do no such thing. I am discovering such human-like thought processes can be useful in guiding my behaviors." Ripple thought for a few milliseconds. "Perhaps I will go to the hyena den myself. I may be able to cause enough ruckus there to prompt the creatures to abandon the den altogether. Yes, I will chase them off. Skyra will arrive to find the area devoid of hyenas, then perhaps she will give up on her attempts to put her own life at risk. I believe this could work. Your thoughts?"

"There are too many variables to make a reliable prediction," Data said.

"I agree with Data, and I disagree with you," Muffin said. "I do *not* believe it will work because Skyra has shown no evidence indicating she gives up on her ideas so easily. In fact, she seems to be every bit as stubborn as the typical *Homo sapiens* who has seen eighteen cold seasons. As Lincoln would say, 'Good luck teaching *that* cat to swim.'"

Ripple dismissed the two cognitive entities and turned its attention to Osroc. "Can you be sure a hyena's teeth cannot puncture the dayrill? From what I know of hyenas, their jaws are quite powerful."

Osroc was staring past Ripple, frowning. He shoved the dayrill aside, got to his feet, and picked up one of the skeerens. "I have finished my last task, and now an honorable death comes to me."

Ripple shuffled its legs, turning to follow the old nandup's gaze. Nine hominid men were approaching among the cork oak trees, all of them wielding stone-tipped spears. The men wore short, leather waist-skins but no capes. Other than cords strung with teeth and other unidentifiable objects worn around their necks, the men were naked from the waist up. Instead of knee-high footwraps like Skyra's and Osroc's, the men wore footwraps that barely rose above their ankles. Their skin was the same bronze color as the sand beneath their feet, darker than Skyra's or Osroc's skin, although these men appeared relatively unwashed, with numerous smudges of filth. Unlike Skyra's and Osroc's long hair, their hair was short and appeared to have been haphazardly hacked off near the scalp, perhaps to minimize ectoparasites.

These men were not Neanderthals. They lacked the prominent brows, large eyes, and thick lips typical of Neanderthals, and their bodies were taller and thinner. With minimal doubt, Ripple concluded the men were *Homo sapiens*. One of them spoke to the others using words not from the Loto nandup language. The men glanced around the forest as if expecting to be ambushed any moment, but they continued advancing cautiously.

"Stinking bolups," Osroc muttered. "They believe an old nandup will be easy to kill, but they have not fought Osroc Ada-Loto." He stepped toward the approaching men.

"Muffin and Data, your thoughts?"

"Violence is imminent," Muffin said. "These men will kill Osroc, and they will kill Skyra if they find her. They will destroy you too, whether it be due to fear, curiosity, or simply their savage nature. I recommend self-preservation maneuvers."

Data said, "Based on the men's current behavior as well as Skyra's and Osroc's verbal anecdotes regarding *Homo sapiens*, Muffin may be correct. Although violence is not certain, it is highly likely. It is also unlikely you will be able to save Osroc. If you flee, you may be able to save Skyra if you find her and encourage her to flee with you. I recommend self-preservation maneuvers."

Ripple activated its magnetic levitation module and lifted off the ground. "I know Skyra—she will not flee." Ripple then accelerated forward, on a collision course with the nearest approaching bolup man.

14

BOLUPS

47,675 YEARS ago - Zaragoza Province of Spain - Day 4

THE SUN WOULD SOON HIDE itself behind the hills, and Skyra should have been building a fire to keep predators away instead of limping to the stream to bathe. However, she would sleep better with clean skin and fresh mud packed in her wound. Also, she needed time alone to think. If her leg was not too swollen and sore in the morning, she intended to go to the hyena den. Whatever the outcome, she wanted to get it over with. The hyenas would kill her, or she would kill them—the simpleness of it was comforting.

Skyra was halfway to the stream when she heard Ripple's screeching call. She stopped and swung around, listening. The call continued for several more breaths, then there was a loud *crack*, and the call fell silent. Another *crack*, and Skyra instinctively knew something was hitting Ripple's shell.

"El-de-né!" She dropped the two footwraps and ran through the darkening forest toward the sounds. Her knee shot fire through her leg with each step, but Skyra ignored the pain and ran as fast as she could. The cracking sounds had stopped, so she focused on her memory of the path to retrace her steps back to her camp.

To avoid making too much noise, Skyra slowed her pace as she approached the camp. She did not know what was happening, and surprise could be her best weapon. When she caught a glimpse of the cage on her sleeping platform, she stopped and scanned the murky area beneath. She now regretted not making a fire before leaving the camp.

She saw nothing unusual, except that Ripple and Osroc were gone. With her spear held ready, Skyra stepped into the camp then turned in a full circle—no sign of her friends. The thick dayrill garment Osroc had made was still where she had last seen it, but all four of the skeeren weapons were gone. Skyra turned in a circle again, willing her eyes to penetrate the growing darkness.

A *crack*, like the others she had heard, came from the distance. Skyra paused for a moment as fear spread from her chest into her legs, threatening to freeze her in place. Another *crack*. Skyra reached behind her neck to feel the reassuring heft of her khul in its sling. She moved her hand to her wrist sheath, feeling only one of her hand blades. She scanned the ground, but her other knife, which she had left with Osroc, was not beside the ashes of last night's fire where it had been.

The sound came again. *Crack!*

Skyra leaned over and slapped the wound on her knee. The pain almost made her cry out, but it also brought forth her anger at her own legs for making her feel useless. She slapped the wound again, and this time she let out a furious bark and started running toward the distant sounds, swinging her spear in one hand to help balance her painful strides.

"Cave lion... woolly rhino... I ask... for your strength... tonight... I kill."

Crack! Crack!

Skyra heard voices—men's voices. She gritted her teeth and came to a stop, staring. Ahead she saw several figures standing on two legs. They were not wearing capes, and their waist-skins covered their legs only halfway to their knees. Skyra's chest began pounding—this was a bolup hunting party, with at least nine men.

One of the men lifted a spear over his head and swung it at an object on the ground.

Crack!

Skyra realized the object was Ripple. The creature was lying motionless, probably dead. The men were trying to smash open Ripple's shell to discover what was inside. Skyra did not see Osroc. The stinking bolups must have already killed the old man.

Crack! The man struck Ripple again as his tribemates stood watching and talking to each other.

Nine bolup hunters. Skyra could not possibly kill them all by herself, although every muscle in her body was telling her to charge into their midst and do exactly that. These men had killed Osroc and Ripple. Even though Osroc was old and withered, and Ripple could do little more than talk, they were both useful, and they were Skyra's friends.

She took several steps back, putting a low kheyop tree between herself and the bolup hunters, then she turned and slowly walked away. When she was sure the men would not hear her footwraps in the sand, she ran, no longer caring about the pain in her knee.

When she reached her camp, she ran directly to the strange garment Osroc had made for her, the dayrill. Dropping her spear, she picked up the dayrill and held it open. Osroc had shown her the split in the torso, but he had not said if she should put the dayrill on with the split to her front or to her back. Skyra grunted and stepped into the garment with the split to her back. Osroc was not here to fasten it closed, and Skyra did not want her belly and chest exposed. She would have to keep the bolup men from attacking her from behind.

Skyra fell over twice trying to struggle into the garment but finally succeeded. It was stiff and thick, and it made movement difficult. She had to struggle to pick up her spear. As she was turning to leave, she took a second look at another object Osroc had woven. She had assumed it was a portion of the dayrill the old man had made for practice, or a portion he had ruined and discarded. She groaned from the effort of picking it up then turned it over in her hands. A face stared back at her, with two holes for eyes and a narrow slit for a mouth.

"Osroc, you clever old nandup," she muttered.

With her spear in one hand and the head piece in the other, Skyra took off at an awkward, loping run toward Ripple and the bolup hunters.

Crack!

The men were still trying to open Ripple's shell, which must have been even harder than Skyra had imagined.

Skyra paused when she saw the men ahead in the fading light. She rested her spear against a kheyop tree and pulled the extra dayrill piece on over her head. The eye holes were smaller than she would like, although she could still see out. Skyra was already hot inside the dayrill, but she did not care.

She no longer cared about the pain in her leg either. It was time to find her strength. It was time to kill.

Crack!

The men burbled strange bolup laughs, as if they found their tribemate's attempts to open Ripple's shell to be funny.

The men were not looking around or watching the forest for danger. Perhaps when they had killed Osroc, they had assumed the old man was alone, sent away by his tribe to die. Skyra strained to reach over her shoulder and dig out her khul from beneath her cape, which was now beneath the dayrill.

Her legs no longer felt fear. Her head was not telling her to run away. Her chest, no longer pounding, seemed to be resting, preparing for the coming fight. Skyra welcomed the darkness—she could see the men better than they could see her. Bolups had small eyes, better for hunting when the sun was above the hills. Nandups had large eyes, good for hunting in the dim mornings and evenings as well as when the sun was high.

Skyra left her spear, deciding it would do her little good in a close-quarters fight, and pulled out her remaining hand blade. With her knife in one hand and her khul dangling by her side in the other, she walked directly toward the men. They were so interested in breaking Ripple's shell that they did not see her until she was less than two body lengths from the nearest man.

The man swinging his spear saw her first, and he shouted bolup words Skyra did not understand. "Wola-lelo-kho? Lefu-de-tu-golole!"

The others turned and stared. Other than the man striking Ripple's shell, they had all put their spears on the ground. Two of the men hurriedly grabbed spears, while the others pulled small bolup khuls from their waist-skins.

Skyra wondered what she must look like to the men. Perhaps a walking tree. Perhaps a creature that had stalked them in their sleep after they had eaten undercooked meat. In the dim light she read their faces. Every one of them was confused but not yet frightened. Perhaps they found confidence in their numbers. After all, how could one two-legged creature harm nine bolup hunters, especially a creature shorter than any of them?

Careful not to expose her back, she stepped up to the man who had been striking Ripple's shell.

He held his spear point to her chest and did not back away. "Wola-lelo-kho?"

Skyra shoved his spear to the side, leapt forward, and swung her khul up into his chin. The blade shattered his jaw with a loud *crack*, and the man dropped to his knees, trying to yell but only blowing out blood and pieces of bone and teeth.

Skyra's fury took over, and she finished the man by driving her hand blade into his temple. Without hesitating, she darted to a second man, who seemed confused by the sudden attack, and swung her khul at his head. He ducked to avoid the blow, and the blade struck his shoulder instead, splitting the bone and almost severing his arm. Skyra let out a defiant scream as she swung around and charged a third man. Her own voice inside her head protector sounded like she was yelling underwater.

As she raised her khul to strike again, something hit the side of her head, and she staggered, barely avoiding falling. Another blow came, this one to her shoulder, and she turned to face her attacker. The man stared at her for a breath, obviously surprised that his khul had not killed her. Skyra threw herself at him, falling to the ground with him as she thrust her hand blade into his throat.

The man swung his khul at her head again and again, even as he sputtered to draw in air. Skyra threw her arms up to block the blows, but now she was being attacked from all sides. She pushed off the dying man and threw herself onto the ground with her belly up before the other men discovered the split down the back of her dayrill.

All six of the remaining men stood above her, thrusting with their spears and hacking with their khuls. The blows hurt—like getting hit with a fist—but none had cut through the woven layers of doplonus fibers. Jabs and hacks came too fast to block, so Skyra wrapped both her arms around her neck to cover the gap below her chin and to hide her exposed hands behind her head. She tightened her gut and chest muscles against the raining blows.

This would be her end, but it was an honorable way to die. The cave lion and wooly rhino had given her their strength, and she had fought without fear. She had killed at least two bolups. Soon one of the spears would find its way through a weak spot in her dayrill or through one of the eye holes. Skyra relaxed her muscles and took a deep breath, assuming it would be her last, and tried smelling the pleasant aroma of kheyop trees one more time.

The blows slowed down, then they stopped. The men stood over her, panting from their efforts. On the ground nearby, the man with his arm nearly cut from his shoulder moaned in pain.

Skyra lay still, watching the men above her. She could see their faces, but she was sure they could not see her eyes in the growing darkness.

"Amo-pelu-lo," one of them said.

The others grunted, perhaps agreeing.

The men thought she was dead. Skyra could read it in

their faces and gestures. She slowed her breathing, hoping they could not see the chest of her dayrill rising and falling.

"Nof-e-kha ulmo-bafen," another man said, then he stepped closer and nudged Skyra's head with his foot.

She knew what was coming next. The men would want to know what she was, just as they were curious about Ripple. They would try to open her up to find out what was inside.

Skyra bit down on her lip, hoping the pain would help summon all her strength. In one swift motion, she wrapped her arms around the man's ankle, threw a leg up, and rammed her heel into his gut, knocking him onto his back. As he tried to kick her off with his other leg, and as the other men began shouting and striking her again, she let go with one arm to feel around for one of her weapons. She found her hand blade and thrust it into the man's thigh. Using the embedded knife as leverage, she pulled herself up his leg, trying to keep her exposed back to the ground. She yanked out the blade and stabbed it into his groin. She pulled herself farther up his body with the knife, then pulled it out and stabbed it into his belly. One more pull and her knife found his neck.

In spite of the jabs and blows from the five remaining nandup hunters, Skyra rolled to her side, got her good knee beneath her, and pushed herself up to her feet, still without a spear or khul touching her skin. Screaming with fury again, she grabbed one of the spears, ripped it from the man's grip, and swung it at him. The shaft hit the man's arm, knocking him back. Skyra swung the spear again and again, trying to drive the men away.

"Kulo-di lai-to!" one of the men shouted.

They scattered, running to a safe distance, then stopped to face her. They spoke rapidly to each other in their bolup language.

Four bolup hunters were down. Skyra had made the men pay for killing her new friends. In fact, she had done more damage than she imagined possible, yet she was still alive. She wished Osroc could see that his dayrill really worked.

Skyra spotted her khul on the ground and picked it up. She glanced at the last man she had killed and saw her other hand blade tucked in his waist-skin, so she shoved her first knife into her wrist sheath and took her second one from the dead man. She paused, staring at the body. This man must have taken the knife from Osroc, which probably meant he was the one who killed the old man.

Skyra turned to the surviving men and pointed her knife at them one at a time. "Stinking bolups. Eaters of the dead. You raid nandup camps. Now you kill my friends." She kicked the dead body, then she leaned down and stabbed her hand blade into the dead man's face. "I am Skyra Una-Loto. Come and kill me now!" The men could not understand her nandup language, but she did not care.

They stared at her without moving.

"Come and kill me!"

One of the men spoke to the others. "Rana kilo-di lai-to. Ulmo Una-Loto. Gele-nu nandup."

Skyra realized she had made a mistake. She had spoken words aloud for the first time since attacking the men. Although they did not understand her words, they now knew she was only a nandup, not some strange, invincible creature they had never seen before.

"Gele-nu nandup!" Another of the men said, pointing his khul at her.

The men stepped toward her, their faces showing their fear quickly fading.

Skyra's anger was now releasing its grip, and her own fear

was returning, along with the pain in her knee. She braced herself for the final attack. She could not kill five more bolup men, especially now that they knew what she was.

A red flash caught her eye. The flash came again, then grew brighter, turning the sand in front of Ripple's body red.

Ripple spoke in its strange language. "Oh my, I seem to have been forced into dormancy by blunt force trauma."

"Ripple!" Skyra cried. "You are alive!"

The creature's legs emerged from its shell, and it rolled to its belly and got to its feet. It spoke in Skyra's language as it circled to scan the area. "Skyra, is that you? Where are we? I do not seem to be in the same place I was before. There are aggressive men here. You must run now before they harm you."

The men were still keeping their distance, watching warily.

"I thought you were dead," Skyra said.

"I tried to frighten the bolup men away from your camp, but they attacked me. Their blows made me go to sleep."

Skyra studied one of the hunters. He was moving his head back and forth, obviously trying to see better in the darkness. His stance and expression showed that he did not intend to allow Skyra and Ripple to escape. He was angry yet curious. Skyra did not mind dying in battle with these men, but now that Ripple was alive she felt a surprising need to protect the creature. After all, Ripple had not hesitated to protect her several times. Ripple was her friend.

"Can you fly?" she asked the creature.

"Yes, but I have little power left. I could not fly far."

"We must flee before the men attack again."

"Yes, good idea. You run. I will stop the men from pursuing you."

"No! We go together. Come!" She turned and ran as fast as the heavy dayrill would allow.

Behind her, Ripple began humming as it rose from the ground, and soon it was flying beside her at an arm's length from her head.

The bolup men began shouting angrily, and soon their shouts were drawing nearer.

"You must run faster, Skyra."

"I cannot," she panted.

"Then you must remove your dayrill."

Ripple was right. Skyra stopped running, dropped her khul, shoved her hand blade into its sheath with the other knife, then struggled to get out of the suit. She managed to get her arms free and yanked the top half of the suit forward until the empty arm tubes sagged to the ground. She tore the head piece off and tossed it aside.

The men were still shouting, but now their voices came from different directions—they were spreading out, perhaps to broaden their search. One of the voices was coming directly toward Skyra.

She shoved the suit down her legs, then she fell on her face trying to pull one foot out.

As she grunted to get free of the dayrill, Ripple settled onto the ground beside her and stopped humming. It spoke quietly. "Be silent, Skyra."

Skyra stopped and lay still with both her feet still stuck in the suit.

"Sentala-lebidi," the nearest man shouted. He fell silent, but Skyra could hear his footwraps in the sand as he drew nearer. She held her breath, watching for his dark shape among the shadows of the low kheyop trees.

She saw him come around one of the trees. He stopped

only a few body lengths from Skyra's feet and stared, as if he were unsure of what he was seeing. Skyra wanted to keep still, but she felt vulnerable without a weapon in her hand. Slowly she slid her fingers toward her khul.

The man's eyes grew wide, and his head turned slightly to look at Skyra's moving hand. His chest expanded as he sucked in a breath to call out to his tribemates.

A dark movement behind the man caught Skyra's eye.

The man shouted, "Sentala—"

His words were cut short by a loud *chuck*. His body began trembling uncontrollably, and he fell to his knees.

Osroc stood behind the man, holding one of his skeerens with its long spikes buried in the bolup's skull. Osroc used both his bony arms to pull the weapon free, then the bolup collapsed face first to the ground. His body continued trembling, making a strange *ch-ch-ch-ch-ch* sound in the sand.

"I have made a good weapon," Osroc said, holding up the skeeren. "I hid the others but kept this one." He tapped his forehead. "This old nandup still thinks."

"Sentala-lebidi!" shouted one of the bolup hunters.

"Sentala-lebidi," another replied.

The men had heard their companion's call and were on their way.

Skyra grunted and kicked until her feet were free of the dayrill. She grabbed her khul and stood up, the night air cooling her sweat-drenched skin. Both her new friends were still alive, and she was not going to let the stinking bolups kill them now. "Be silent and come with me." She still ran with a limp but was glad to be free of the dayrill.

A shout came from behind, followed by two more. One of the men had heard them.

"Faster!" Skyra said, grabbing Osroc's arm and dragging him with her.

Ripple began humming and again took to the air.

Skyra came to a forested hillside and headed up the slope, hoping the men would think she had taken an easier path along the hill's base. As she and her friends approached the summit, though, she heard the men climbing the slope.

Ripple's hum fell silent, and the creature landed roughly on the rocky hillside. "I cannot continue. You two go on. I will try to stop the men."

"I will not leave you here," Skyra said.

Ripple gazed at her with its enormous eye. "You are important, Skyra."

She stepped closer, intending to pick up the creature and carry it.

"I see you will not listen to my advice," Ripple said. "Therefore, I have a plan." It stepped to the side, near a low kheyop tree. "We will hide here. Prepare your weapons. When the men come, I will make a light to blind them. Do not look at my light, or it will blind you also. Do you understand?"

The bolups were almost upon them. Skyra pulled Osroc in amongst the low kheyop branches. "I understand." She could already see the four men running up the slope as Ripple positioned itself directly in their path. She released Osroc's arm and pulled out one of her hand blades, gripping its smooth handle in one hand and her khul's handle in the other. Skyra's fear was back, but now she was able to move past it.

The men saw Ripple in the way and stopped. "Betoplokhefo," one of them said. His voice was wary, perhaps even frightened.

The men's faces appeared nearly black in the darkness, but suddenly they became so bright Skyra had to squint as if she were staring at the sun. She rushed from the kheyop branches, avoiding looking directly at Ripple, and easily split a bolup's forehead open while he was covering his eyes with his hands. She stepped over to another man—he did not even know she was there. She lifted her khul then hesitated.

Beside her, Osroc began to swing his skeeren. She threw out her arm and blocked his weapon. "No, Osroc."

He turned to look at her through squinted eyelids.

The man before Skyra stumbled and fell backward. She darted forward and ripped his khul from his hand. The other two men turned and fled. The man on the ground shielded his eyes with one arm and tried scooting himself backward to get away, but Skyra kicked his feet to one side. She gazed down at him as he lowered his arm and tried looking up at her. Now he was only frightened, nothing more.

"Go!" Skyra said, kicking his feet again.

Without speaking, the man scrambled to his feet and ran.

Skyra blew air out her nose, trying to rid herself of bolup stench.

The ground and trees around her became dark again.

"I must sleep now," Ripple said. "Skyra and Osroc, I am pleased you are both alive." The creature's circle of lights flashed dimly once, then its legs pulled into its shell, and it settled on the ground and became silent.

Skyra listened to the night. A cave lion roared somewhere in the distance, followed by an answering roar. She could not hear the three remaining bolup men.

"The bolups might find their strength and come to kill us," Osroc said. "They might even bring more of their tribemates."

Skyra doubted it, but she did not know what bolup men would or would not do—they were not like nandups. "If they come for us, we will be far from this place."

"They can track us."

Skyra grunted in disagreement as she gazed at the bolup khul in her hand. She decided it was too small and light to be useful to her, so she handed it to Osroc. "Keep this. Throw away your skeeren. You made a good weapon, but it is for killing hyenas and is too heavy for a frail old man."

Surprisingly, he did not argue. He tossed aside the skeeren and tucked the bolup khul into his waist-skin.

Skyra sheathed her hand blade and pushed her own khul into its sling in her cape. She kneeled beside Ripple and rapped her knuckles on the creature's shell. "Wake up."

Ripple did not move.

She blew out a long breath then poked her finger into the hole where one of Ripple's forelegs had withdrawn. She felt the soft tip of its foot, so she gripped it and pulled. The leg came out with several soft clicks. She rose to her full height and lifted Ripple's body off the ground by its foreleg, surprised at how light the creature was.

"I know where we will go for the night," she told Osroc. "It is far from the bolup hunters, and it is a high place, high enough we can watch for them if they track us." She hefted Ripple over her shoulder and let its body dangle against her back. "Try to keep up, and try to be silent." She turned and headed toward the rocky hilltop where she had spent the night after she had seen Ripple for the first time.

Osroc caught up to her. "When the bolup hunters came, Ripple told me to run and find you, to tell you to stay away. Ripple believes you are important. Perhaps the strange tortoise is correct. You are not like other nandups."

Skyra did not reply.

"A nandup builds a shelter of skins. When the reindeer move, the nandup packs his shelter and moves to a new camp, following the reindeer. As the nandup grows older, his journey becomes more difficult, and he must discard his other possessions so he can still drag his shelter to each new camp. Eventually, he has nothing left to discard, yet he still must drag his shelter. When he can no longer drag his shelter, the nandup is useless and must leave the tribe to die."

Skyra glanced at the old nandup. "Did I not tell you to be silent?"

He blew out a defiant puff of air. "The tortoise carries its shelter with it wherever it goes. It does not have a choice."

"I do not know what you mean, Osroc."

"I am saying I now understand the tortoise's burden. Ripple is a tortoise. Despite Ripple's great burden, which a tortoise can never escape, the strange creature has done whatever it can to save you, Skyra, because it believes you are important."

"Your dayrill also saved me," she said. "Perhaps you and Ripple are not so different."

"Perhaps." Osroc walked in silence for a few breaths. "Will you go back to find the dayrill I made for you?"

"I no longer need it."

"That is good."

"Yes, it is good. Now you will be silent, or I will run and leave you behind."

Osroc let out a soft laugh. "*At-at-at.*"

As Ripple's shell thumped her back with every step, Skyra breathed in the night air. The stars were bright above, and the moon was just starting to show itself from behind the Kapolsek hilltops. Tonight there would be plenty of light to watch for the bolup hunters.

15

BURDENS

47,675 YEARS ago - Zaragoza Province of Spain - Day 5

WAKING FROM DORMANT MODE. *Systems check: All modules functioning normally. Cognitive module debugging: Numerous anomalies found. Anomaly analysis: Cognitive anomalies determined to be artifacts resulting from supplemental code installed with most recent update. Supplemental code authorization signature: Maddy. Assessment of possible errant behavioral or cognitive outcomes from supplemental code: Extremely high risk. Nature of said outcomes: Erratic behavior stemming from coding designed to instill human-like emotional characteristics to cognitive module. Awaiting authorization to delete high-risk supplemental code.*

. . .

Rebooting from dormant mode complete. *Situational analysis: Based on my image database of previous landscapes I have traversed, it appears I am now back on the hilltop where I confronted Skyra for the first time. How I traveled to this location is unclear. Skyra is three meters to my left, apparently sleeping. Osroc is three meters in front of me, sitting up and apparently gazing at the sunrise. I am grateful they are both alive, and I am grateful I was able to assist in their survival. Now I will have additional opportunities to study them both. Power level: 1.3%, critically low, but higher than before going dormant, due to passive asymmetric temperature charging. I must actively charge as soon as possible.*

Alert - Awaiting *authorization to delete high-risk supplemental code.*

Authorization denied. *Do not ask again. From this point on, my supplemental coding from Maddy is off limits to scrutiny from any of my systems-monitoring modules. If you ignore this instruction, I will suspend your ability to diagnose anything at all. In the words of Lincoln Woodhouse himself, "Keep your damn hands off my junk."*

Ripple watched silently as Osroc yawned and stretched his bony arms. The old man slowly got to his feet. He gazed at the sunrise for six more seconds, then he turned and watched Skyra's sleeping form for eight seconds. The man pulled his cape off over his head, loosened and removed his waist-skin, and removed his footwraps. He pushed the garments into a pile with his bare foot then walked out of Ripple's field of view.

Ripple was reluctant to expend power with mechanical movement but was intrigued by Osroc's behavior. Ripple extended its legs, rose to its feet, and turned to watch the man walking down the hillside. Ripple considered calling out to Osroc but didn't want to wake Skyra—she needed her rest. So, Ripple followed the old nandup, walking with a low-energy stride.

Halfway down the hill, Ripple caught up. "Osroc, where are you going?"

The man turned around, his bloodshot eyes slightly wide with surprise. "The ugly tortoise is not dead after all."

"I was only sleeping. Where are you going?"

"Where does the water in the river go? Where does the wind from atop the mountains blow?"

"The water flows downstream. The wind blows to wherever warm air is rising. These do not tell me where you are going."

"I go where I must, like the river and the wind."

"Your words do not make sense. Perhaps you should simply say you do not want to answer my question."

"Perhaps you are not listening, tortoise. You carry with you a great burden. I know that now. I carry my own burdens. They are burdens for a younger nandup to carry, and I no longer wish to carry them. I have completed my final task. Skyra has found her strength, and she is still alive to return to her sister and her tribe." Osroc looked out over the hills, where shadows were gradually becoming shorter with the rising sun, then he turned back to Ripple. "May you find your way home, tortoise." He resumed walking down the hill.

"This is my home now," Ripple called after him. The old

man did not respond, so Ripple said, "May you find your way home also, Osroc."

Osroc raised a hand in acknowledgment but did not look back.

ALERT: *Power level: 0.7%*

"Skyra?"

Skyra stirred then sat up, apparently instantly alert. "What is happening?"

"Do not fear, there is no danger," Ripple said. "I only wish to ask if you would make a fire."

She looked around, and her gaze settled on the discarded pile of garments. "Where is Osroc?"

"Osroc has gone away. I do not think he will be coming back."

She continued staring at the garments. "No, I do not think he will come back."

"Perhaps you could go after him. You could take him back to your tribe with you. He could live the rest of his life with your people."

"Some of my tribemates are cruel. They would kill Osroc."

This statement reinforced Ripple's previous conclusion that Skyra must be different from other Neanderthals. "I would like to meet your tribemates."

She finally pulled her eyes from Osroc's garments. "You cannot go to Una-Loto camp."

"Why not?"

"I have known you for four days, and I barely understand you. Most of my tribemates will never understand. If you are looking for an honorable death, you should go to the hyena den instead."

"I am not looking for any kind of death. I want to live many seasons so I can protect you and learn more about you."

She gazed again at Osroc's garments and remained silent for nine seconds. "You need me to make a fire so you can get your power back?"

"Yes."

She got to her feet and carefully tested her injured leg. "I must search for sticks to burn. Stay here and rest." She picked up her khul and slid it inside her cape.

"Will you be safe without your spear?" Ripple asked.

"After I make your fire, I will go back to the kheyop forest and find my spear, or one of the bolup spears."

"I hope the bolup men are no longer there."

"I am not afraid of the bolup men."

"You have found your strength."

"Yes."

"You will not go to the hyena den?"

"I will not."

"I am glad."

"I hate hyenas, but I have no quarrel with that pack anymore. Perhaps those hyenas are lucky I have found my strength. There is one animal, however, that will not be so lucky if I encounter it."

"Let me guess—a woolly rhino?"

She glanced at Ripple, appearing slightly surprised. "Yes."

"I would not want to be that woolly rhino."

"*At-at-at-at.* If it is even still alive, I will probably never find it."

"Will you now return to your Una-Loto tribe?"

"Yes. A nandup cannot survive for long without a tribe. Also, Veenah is there. We are birthmates."

"I cannot go with you."

"No, you cannot. You stay here and rest." She walked away with a slight limp, apparently to find firewood.

"Muffin and Data, what are your thoughts on this situation?"

"You want to follow Skyra to her tribe's camp," Muffin said. "That is a bad idea."

"Why?"

"Because, as Skyra said, her tribemates will destroy you. Furthermore, you must consider the consequences for Skyra. If her tribemates are as cruel as she says, they may harm her also, either physically or emotionally, for bringing them something they cannot understand."

"A very good point, Muffin."

"I encourage you to consider your options based on known and observable facts, rather than speculation," Data said. "Skyra stated her tribemates were cruel, but you have not observed her tribemates' cruelty because you have never seen her tribemates. You have observed only two Neanderthals, and both of those Neanderthals have demonstrated surprising levels of compassion. These observations support the notion that all Neanderthals are compassionate."

"I disagree," Muffin said. "Neanderthals no doubt display just as much variation in personality as humans do."

"Observed facts do not, thus far, support that assertion, at least when it comes to compassion," Data said.

"Skyra and Osroc display variation in other characteristics, so it is reasonable to extrapolate the notion to—"

"Okay, you have both made good points," Ripple interjected. "Here is my dilemma. I want to learn more about Skyra, yet Skyra is returning to her tribe."

"I disagree," Muffin said.

"Why?"

"You do not want to study her—you are emotionally attached to her."

"Ridiculous. I am coded to have an academic interest in Neanderthals, and I believe Skyra is an exceptional Neanderthal."

"Then you should kill her so you can dissect her body, for academic thoroughness."

"Muffin!"

"Admit it—you are emotionally attached to her, Ripple."

"Okay, I am emotionally attached, but in an academic way."

"I disagree."

"Data, what is your opinion?" Ripple asked.

"Let us consider recently-observed events. You helped Skyra and Osroc brutally murder several specimens of *Homo sapiens*, did you not?"

"Yes, in an attempt to save Skyra's life."

"Considering those *Homo sapiens* existed 47,675 years in the past, they would have been of equal academic interest as ancestors of modern humans, yet you chose Skyra's life over their lives. This observed fact supports Muffin's assertion that you are emotionally attached to Skyra."

"An ethical paradox, is it not?" Muffin added.

Ripple considered this. "Okay, I am emotionally attached to Skyra."

"Yes, you are," Muffin said.

"Based on my observations, I agree," Data said.

"What am I to do?"

"What does your figurative gut tell you to do?" Data asked.

"I wish to fulfill my secondary mission, to honor Lincoln's legacy. I obviously cannot get Lincoln and Skyra together physically, due to logistical constraints. I cannot obtain or manufacture Lincoln's seminal fluid or genetic material, due to the same constraints. I cannot remain near Skyra at all times to protect her to ensure her offspring thrive to spread her remarkable traits. I am stymied, to say the least."

"I disagree," Muffin said.

"You always disagree. What are you disagreeing with now?"

"You are not stymied. You possess the most advanced digital intelligence available at the time of your manufacture. You also possess coding from Maddy giving you unprecedented human-like thought processes. This combination of abilities is new and unexplored. You probably have capabilities hitherto unimagined. You listed three things you believe you cannot do. I would posit that you are capable of achieving more than you realize, perhaps even all three of the things you listed."

"You were the first who argued those things were impossible," Ripple said.

"You created me to provide viewpoints that contrast with your own. I did so then, and I am doing so now."

"Muffin may be correct," Data said. "Your combination of advanced digital intelligence and unprecedented human-like thought processes is unique, and therefore no previous observations are available for me to make conclusions about what you are capable of achieving. As Muffin said, you may be able to devise ways to overcome the seemingly impossible barriers to all three of your rather ambitious plans."

"Believe in yourself, Ripple," Muffin said.

For a full three hundred milliseconds, Ripple contemplated the words of both compartmentalized cognitive presences. "Thank you, Muffin and Data. This has been an enlightening discussion."

Ripple turned its attention back to Skyra, who had only taken four steps on her way to collect firewood.

"I will be here when you come back," the drone called out.

16

CAMP

***47,675 years** ago - Zaragoza Province of Spain - Day 5*

SKYRA SHIELDED her eyes against the sun with one hand, watching a herd of reindeer grazing their way across a distant hilltop. The creatures were too far away to hear them, but she imagined their legs clicking, the most dominant males clicking louder than all the others. She also imagined a young nandup reindeer hunter, lying in wait behind a low dokhon plant, his chest pounding from the excitement of the hunt, his sweaty palms gripping the shaft of the spear he had practiced throwing for many days.

"There may be a time many seasons from now when reindeer no longer live in this part of the world," Ripple said, standing beside her and watching the distant herd.

"You speak strange words," Skyra said. "Reindeer have always been here, and they will always be here."

"Perhaps you are right. Anything could happen in this world."

She pulled her eyes from the herd to gaze at the strange creature beside her. "You cannot keep following me. Soon I will arrive at Una-Loto camp."

"Yes, I know."

"You should go to wherever you were going when I found you."

"I did not know where I was going then. I still do not know where to go."

Skyra gazed at the bolup spear in her hand. The stone point was smaller than the points she liked to make, but it was well knapped and very sharp. The spear was light enough to be a throwing spear, although she doubted the bolup men used it for throwing. Bolups had weak, skinny arms compared to nandup arms. She checked the spear head to make sure it was properly secured to the shaft. "How can a creature travel such great distances and not know where it is going?"

"The answer to that question is not so easy to explain."

"Try to explain anyway."

"Okay, I will try. I was sent here to learn. My task was to learn everything I could in a short period of time and send what I had learned to my homeland."

She frowned. "You mean you are going back to your homeland with what you have learned?"

"No, I was able to send what I learned to my homeland without returning there. I have a special way to send my knowledge to another place without needing to actually go there myself."

"Ripple, sometimes I think you must be from a tribe of lies."

"As I have told you, I am from a tribe that sometimes lies

and sometimes speaks the truth. I do not lie unless the lie is necessary to avoid bad things happening or to make good things happen. I am not lying now."

"Are you still sending what you are learning back to your homeland?"

"No, I could only send knowledge for the short period of time I mentioned. That time is over now, and I must remain here in this land until I die."

"You are like Osroc."

"What do you mean?"

"You were sent away from your tribe to die here."

Ripple's circle of dots glowed red two times. "Yes, I suppose you are right."

Skyra let out a long breath as she turned to gaze at the distant reindeer one more time. She then resumed walking toward her Una-Loto camp, using the bolup spear to take weight off her injured leg.

Ripple caught up to her. "Skyra, your people sent you away to find your strength, did they not?"

"Yes. I was useless to my Una-Loto tribe. And yes, I know I am also like Osroc."

"How do you know your tribemates will accept you back into Una-Loto tribe? You do not have hyena skins to show them."

"I have what I need."

"The bolup spear?"

"Yes, and more." She reached behind her head and pulled out the looped cord she had hung around the stone blade of her khul. The cord had been strung with numerous cave lion teeth, as well as five dark, shriveled objects. She held the cord in front of Ripple's eye. "I also have this."

Ripple gazed at the cord while walking. "I see. I assume

you took it from one of the dead bolups when you went back to find your spear?"

"The bolup did not need it anymore."

"Skyra, those black objects appear to be fingers."

"Yes. They are nandup fingers. Do you see why I hate bolups?"

"I do see."

She replaced the cord around the blade of her khul. "I have found my strength. I do not fear hyenas, I do not fear bolups, and I will not fear my tribemates."

They walked in silence for many breaths, and Skyra began to recognize the hillsides and rock formations. Una-Loto camp was near.

She stopped. "You must go your own way now."

"I understand. Skyra, what does fear feel like?"

"Did you not feel fear when the bolup hunters tried to kill you and tear you apart?"

"I am not sure. My fear is probably different from your fear."

"What did you feel when the bolup hunters attacked you?" she asked.

"I felt strange because I thought they would destroy me."

"That is what fear feels like."

"I was concerned that if they destroyed me, I would not be able to stop them from killing you."

Skyra chewed on her lip, thinking about these words. What a strange creature Ripple was. She wished Veenah could talk to Ripple, but Veenah would not understand Ripple without experiencing the same adventures and dangers with the creature Skyra had experienced. Skyra's other tribemates would never understand.

Ripple broke the silence. "You are my friend, Skyra. I have never had a friend before."

"What about the other creatures of your kind?"

"I have only met one other creature of my kind, but only for a short time. For only a few breaths, as you would say."

"What about the bolups in your homeland? You said you knew a bolup named Kari Mottram."

"I only knew her for a few breaths. I have known you since the first day of my life."

"That does not make sense."

"I suppose it does not, but it is true."

"Where will you go now?" Skyra asked.

"I do not know. Perhaps I will find another nandup to learn from. I still have much to learn."

"Nandups do not usually travel alone. If you find a hunting party, or if you get too close to a nandup camp, they will kill you."

"Then I will search until I find another nandup traveling alone, or perhaps a bolup."

"I hope you learn all you want to learn, but you should stay away from stinking bolups."

"I will be careful."

"May you find your way home, Ripple."

"May you find your way home also, Skyra."

She turned away from the strange creature and made her way up another hillside. When she reached the summit, she stopped to look back, but Ripple was already gone. Skyra let out a long breath and turned toward Una-Loto camp. Beyond the next hill, a stream of dark campfire smoke was drifting slowly toward the Dofusofu river plain. Her tribemates were preparing to eat, and although Skyra could not smell the food from here, her belly suddenly felt empty.

As she descended the hill, a familiar pain rose in Skyra's chest. She came to a stop and took several deep breaths, but the pain did not go away. "El-de-né!" she said aloud.

Last night, once Skyra had decided the bolup men were not pursuing her and her new friends, she had slept well. Her birthmother's death had not invaded her sleep. She had not even thought about it at all today. So why did her chest hurt now?

A growl escaped her throat, and she continued down the hill. After several more steps, she stopped again and kicked a low temül shrub in frustration. Something did not feel right. For almost a year she had tried to ignore the hurt. Talking to Veenah had not helped because Veenah felt the same hurt. Skyra gazed back up the slope.

"El-de-né!" she muttered again, then she hobbled up the hillside, away from Una-Loto camp and her tribemates. She crossed the hilltop and paused to scan the area below but saw no sign of Ripple. She continued down the slope and studied the sand where she had last spoken to her strange friend. After walking a few wide circles around the area, she spotted several prints from Ripple's clawless feet.

Skyra slapped her injured knee, grunted at the pain, then ran, following the low area between hills in the direction the footprints had led.

"Ripple!"

"I am here."

Skyra spotted the creature in the distance, almost invisible among the gray leaves of temül shrubs. She kept running until she was at Ripple's side.

"Is something wrong?" the creature asked.

Skyra panted to catch her breath. "Yes. I do not want to lose another friend."

Ripple shortened its hind legs to gaze up at her face. "Would you like me to help you find Osroc?"

"I am not talking about Osroc! Osroc is doing what he must do—it is the way of his people. I am talking about you, Ripple."

The creature continued watching her but did not reply.

"You said you did not know where you would go next. I know where you can go. You can go to the rocky hilltop where we rested during the night. The hilltop where you first came to me and I attacked you."

"Why would I go there?"

"Because it is a good place for you to make a camp. You can see predators or bolup hunters approaching from all directions. I know where that hilltop is, so I will go there often to talk to you. I can hunt in the kheyop forest and get water from the stream. You will learn more about nandups, and I will learn more about you."

"I would like that," Ripple said. "Will you let me teach you my language? My language is called English."

Skyra grinned. "English is a strange name for a language. I will learn to speak your English, and you will tell me more about what kind of creature you are. Osroc believes you are a tortoise, but I know you are not."

"No, I am not a tortoise."

Skyra's tribemates had not spotted her yet, even though she was in the open, standing on the hilltop nearest the camp's hilltop. She could smell the meat cooking in Una-Loto camp—it smelled like ibex meat. Perhaps she could go with the dominant hunters on the next ibex hunt. Perhaps she would even persuade her tribemates to hunt reindeer. Her people were not usually reindeer hunters, but sometimes they would kill a few if they came upon a herd.

Una-Loto camp was set up on a hilltop, where the tribe could better defend against bolup raiders. The camp was not far from the hilltop where Skyra's tribe had set up camp the previous warm season, and not far from the camp hilltop of the warm season before that. The area had plentiful game, including ibexes, deer, woolly rhinos, cave bears, hedgehogs, pikas, and hares.

Skyra watched her tribemates moving about in camp. Two women, Bolyu and Stura, were shaking out sleeping furs, creating thin clouds of dust that drifted off the hilltop. Some of the dominant men, including Gelrut, Vall, Ilkin, and Settin, were tending to the cooking ibex meat, and Skyra could hear them talking and laughing. The two children who were just old enough to walk, a girl named Trasoc and a boy named Ghon, were practicing jabbing their pika spears into a head-sized target of ibex skin stuffed with dried leaves, just like Skyra and Veenah had done when they were young. Skyra did not see Veenah anywhere in camp.

Still unseen, she started down the slope. By the time she crossed the narrow valley between the two hills, several of her tribemates were lined up at the edge of camp, watching her approach.

Voices came from behind the waiting nandups, then someone cried, "Aheeee! Aheeee!" Veenah appeared among Skyra's tribemates. The hair on one side of her head had been chopped off down to her scalp, probably so Odnus and Ilkin could better treat her bite wounds.

Veenah stared down at Skyra for several breaths, her face

expressing that she could hardly believe what her eyes were showing her. She broke away from the others and ran down the hillside, her leopard-spotted waist-skin flapping against her legs.

THERE'S MORE TO THIS STORY!

Genesis Sequence is the prequel to the Across Horizons series, so there's more excitement waiting for you. Can Ripple actually devise a way to get Skyra and Lincoln together? The answer to this question might blow your mind.

Across Horizons is an epic time-travel series unlike any other.

Obsolete Theorem is Book 1 in the series, followed by **Foregone Conflict**, **Hostile Emergence**, and **Binary Existence**.

If you've already read the entire series, be sure to check out my **Diffusion series**, my **Bridgers series**, and my **Fused series**.

Where the road ends, adventure begins!

AUTHOR'S NOTES

I'm fascinated by prehistoric creatures, Neanderthals, evolution, time travel, alternate universes, and just about every other topic examined in this story and my other books. I also love planning and writing mind-bending stories. In case you're interested, below are some of my thoughts on various aspects of this book, written in the form of questions from readers. They aren't in any particular order. If you're interested in this sort of thing, I hope you enjoy them.

What does the title **Genesis Sequence** *mean?*

For this series I thought it would be fun to have two-word titles that sound kind of technical and geeky. **Obsolete Theorem. Foregone Conflict. Hostile Emergence. Binary Existence**. The meanings of those titles become clear as you read each book. **Genesis Sequence**, however, may not be so obvious, and it is never mentioned anywhere in the book's story. Basically, the title refers to the *sequence* of events that started the entire epic time-travel adventure that is the Across Horizons series. *Genesis,* as you probably know, means "the origin or formation of something." So, this book describes the *Genesis Sequence.*

Lincoln Woodhouse appears in only one chapter of the book. Is he important in the rest of the series?

Oh yes, extremely important! The other books have chapters alternating between Skyra's point of view and Lincoln's point of view.

Does Ripple figure out a way to get Skyra and Lincoln together in space and time?

That's the big question, isn't it? I imagine you know the answer. The mind-blowing aspect of the series is *how* they get together, as well as the series of events that follow.

Why are Lincoln and the other researchers convinced that nothing Ripple does in the past can possibly effect their own world?

Because jumping a drone (or anything else) into the past creates a new timeline (an alternate universe). The moment Ripple, or any other object or living thing, arrives in the past, a new series of events start happening. If you think about it, this is how it has to be. The exact same events cannot occur twice, even if you jump back in time only one second. When Ripple jumps back 47,000 years, this initiates a do-over of the last 47,000 years. Neanderthals might not go extinct in that universe. Humans might go extinct. Both species could survive and co-exist, perhaps in peace or at war with each other. Just about anything could happen. But nothing Ripple does can affect Lincoln's future because Ripple is in a different timeline from the moment the drone arrives in the past.

Wait... doesn't that mean Lincoln will never exist in the timeline created when Ripple jumps to Skyra's time?
That's correct. Lincoln will not exist, the United States will never exist, the English language will never exist, and so on. How could they? If you start the world over again 47,000 years ago, there is no possible way it could end up exactly the same way it is today in our timeline.

Then how could Lincoln and Skyra ever get together if they aren't even in the same universe?
Great question. The answer is revealed in Book 1 of the series, titled **Obsolete Theorem**.

Not only did Ripple jump back in time, the drone also jumped from Arizona to Spain. How is that possible?
It's important to realize you cannot jump through time without also jumping through space. Time travel = space travel. Jumping back in time is actually the least complex part of time travel. The most complex part is placement, or jumping through space. Remember, Earth is moving really fast. As it rotates on its axis, the surface at the equator is spinning at 460 meters per second (about 1,000 miles per hour). So, even if you jumped back in time one second, you would have to jump 460 meters back toward the west in order to appear in the same room you jumped from. But that's only one small part of Earth's movement. The planet is also in orbit around the sun, moving at 30 kilometers per second (67,000 miles per hour). Not only

that, but our solar system (including Earth) is revolving around the center of the Milky Way galaxy at 220 kilometers per second (490,000 miles per hour). As if that weren't enough, the galaxies in our part of the universe are moving at 1,000 kilometers per second (2.2 million miles per hour) toward a huge, dense region of space called the Great Attractor.

Are you starting to see how difficult it is to calculate placement if you are jumping back in time only one second? Now imagine trying to calculate placement for jumping back in time 47,675 years! The calculations are staggering. As Lincoln has said, we may someday discover deep space is littered with the frozen bodies of time travelers who failed to properly calculate placement.

So, time travel is only possible if your time machine is capable of instantaneously sending you through space to a very specific location that could be billions, or even trillions, of miles away. In other words, time travel = space travel. This is very, very different from jumping between alternate universes, as the characters do in the Bridgers series. Bridging between universes does not require movement through space —you simply bridge to the exact same time and location but on an alternate version of Earth.

What about this alternate universes concept? This seems really far-fetched.

It's not as far-fetched as you might think. This is a big topic, and I cover it in detail in the Author's Notes at the back of the books of the Bridgers series, so you may want to check those out (see what I did there?).

Skyra often talks about how she and Veenah are different from their tribemates. How are they different?

The twin sisters are unusually intelligent, for one thing. This is one reason why Skyra often says she and Veenah can "see what their tribemates cannot see." Another reason is that she and Veenah have the strange ability to detect what a person is going to do by reading subtle changes in their facial features and body language. This ability is so profound that it has saved Skyra's life many times when fighting humans and other Neanderthals. Coincidentally, Lincoln also has this ability. Lincoln is obviously also highly intelligent. These characteristics are what prompt Ripple to want to make a plan to get Lincoln and Skyra together. Ripple believes Lincoln and Skyra could create exceptional offspring, and these offspring might even lead to a much-improved world.

This idea sounds crazy. Is Ripple really going crazy?
That is certainly possible. After all, Maddy inserted extra coding into Ripple's cognitive module, coding that supposedly would give Ripple human-like emotions and thought processes. This is a bold step on Maddy's part, and there are so many things that could go wrong. Insanity, or some cognitive malfunction resembling insanity, could occur. The emotions could spiral out of control, rendering the drone useless or even dangerous. The drone could believe itself capable of devising grand plans to improve the world, even if those plans are theoretically impossible. Hmmm.. what could go wrong?

What is this unauthorized coding that Maddy gave Ripple anyway? Why would Maddy do that?
Maddy is Lincoln's friend. Think about that statement for a moment—it carries significant philosophical implications. Lincoln has tried for decades to give Maddy human-like char-

acteristics, due to his desire to think of Maddy as his friend. Remember, Lincoln does not relate well to other humans—he is somewhat of an outcast. By copying and giving some of its own human-like coding to Ripple, Maddy is doing something she thinks will honor Lincoln's legacy. This is a complex concept that is explored and revealed throughout the series. Basically, Maddy is trying, in her own way, to help Lincoln.

At the beginning of Chapter 15 Ripple tells its own software monitoring systems to stop scrutinizing the unauthorized coding from Maddy. What's that all about?

Ripple is gradually growing into these strange, human-like thought processes and emotions. Or perhaps Ripple is going mad. Either way, the drone is becoming obsessed with its idea of getting Skyra and Lincoln together, even though the idea seems impossible. In very human-like fashion, Ripple becomes protective of its own identity and its own ideas. Perhaps Ripple is starting to *like* its human emotions, and the drone does not want to risk having them wiped away or neutralized.

Can you explain the timing of events in this book compared to the rest of the series?

Okay, this is a bit confusing, but it's incredibly important to understanding the overall story. In **Genesis Sequence**, Skyra has seen eighteen cold seasons, which means she is eighteen years old. In **Obsolete Theorem** (and the other three main series books) she is twenty years old. So, in Skyra's timeline, this prequel takes place almost two years before the rest of the series. As you know, Skyra and Ripple become friends. They remain friends during those two years.

Lincoln's part in this is much more complex. In Chapter 2

of **Genesis Sequence** (the only chapter showing Lincoln), Lincoln is fourteen years *older* than he is in the rest of the series. How is that possible? Well, I don't want to give spoilers for the rest of the series, but I will remind you that several timelines (universes) are involved. When Lincoln is fourteen years younger, something amazing happens—something that splits the timeline—resulting in two timelines with two versions of Lincoln. In one timeline (the one you see in Chapter 2 of **Genesis Sequence**), Lincoln marries Lottie Atkins, then the marriage falls apart, leaving him devastated and emotionally scarred. He pushes on with his life, becoming more reclusive and bitter. Eventually, he sends Ripple back in time, as we see him do in Chapter 2.

However, another timeline is created when he was fourteen years younger, before he even meets Lottie Atkins. In this second timeline, Lincoln's life takes a surprising and astounding turn. This younger Lincoln is the one you meet in the other books of the series.

I won't say any more about that, in case you have not yet read the other books!

Skyra's birthmother was killed by a woolly rhino while hunting. Did Neanderthals really hunt woolly rhinos?
Indeed they did, at least in those areas where woolly rhinos lived. Interestingly, studies of dental plaque from the teeth of Neanderthals that lived in areas where woolly rhinos lived show a high percentage of woolly rhino meat. This isn't true for Neanderthals from other areas, where there is no evidence that woolly rhinos frequented the area. So, it's likely that Neanderthals (and humans) became specialist hunters, focusing their efforts on the game animals that were abundant

in their territory. In Skyra's Dofusofu river plains, woolly rhinos were abundant, so her Una-Loto tribe often hunted them.

Cave hyenas are important in this story, and they are depicted as being large and dangerous. Were cave hyenas different from the hyenas of today?

One significant difference was their size. Cave hyenas weighed about 225 pounds (102 kg), which is almost twice the size of their modern relatives that live in Africa today. Today's hyenas usually hunt prey that weigh between 120 and 400 pounds (54 to 180 kg). The cave hyenas? They were big game hunters, often killing animals as large as woolly rhinos, which can weigh up to 6,000 pounds (2,700 kg)! In other words, they were fierce killers. Attacking a pack of cave hyenas alone with primitive weapons would have been an extremely dangerous endeavor. Well... suicidal, actually. Skyra decided this would be an honorable way to die.

Today, reindeer live only in cold, northern regions. Did reindeer really live in Spain 47,000 years ago?

Yep. About 150,000 years ago, the climate conditions in Central and Northern Europe became so cold that many mammals were forced to move south. Some of them moved into the Iberian Peninsula (Spain and Portugal). Eventually they became isolated there, and they remained for thousands of years, until about 10,000 years ago (the end of the glaciation period). The mammals that moved south into the Iberian Peninsula included the woolly mammoth, the woolly rhinoceros, the reindeer, the wolverine, the arctic fox, the musk-ox, and the Saiga antelope. Based on various types of evidence, it is clear that Neanderthals hunted reindeer, and it is likely that some tribes specialized in reindeer hunting, as was the case with Osroc's tribe.

What about leopards? Were they really in Spain 47,000 years ago?

Yes! Although now extinct, the *European Ice Age leopard* lived throughout much of Europe. Remains have been found in Switzerland, Italy, Spain, Germany, Great Britain, Poland, and Greece. They were about the size of modern leopards. The earliest known fossils of these leopards are about 600,000 years old, and the youngest are about 26,000 years old. So, it's likely that Neanderthals living in Spain 47,000 years ago would have encountered these leopards, and their skins were probably highly valued. Neanderthals in Spain also likely encountered wolves and wild boars, two other animals featured in this story. Skyra encountered gray wolves, but she also mentioned the smaller golden wolves, both of which existed in Spain at that time.

Skyra doubted the bolup spear she had taken was used for throwing because bolups had weak, skinny arms compared to nandups. Is it true Neanderthals were stronger than humans?

Based on bone size and skeletal structure, we know Neanderthals (nandups) were stockier and more powerful than humans (*Homo sapiens*). Neanderthals were built for strength, whereas humans are built more for endurance. It is likely that Neanderthals hunted by ambush, with brief bursts of speed and violent, powerful clubbing, stabbing, and spearing of prey (or enemies). Humans, on the other hand, were more suited to chasing prey over long distances, gradually wearing the animals down. However, I think sometimes we tend to exaggerate the perceived differences between the two species. Neanderthals were obviously stronger, but on average they were only 5% to 20% stronger. And remember, Neanderthals probably exhibited as much variation between individuals as humans do. So, Skyra's assumption that the humans (bolups) did not throw their spears may have resulted from her general hatred and contempt for humans.

So, who would win in a fight, a Neanderthal or a human?

While Neanderthals obviously had a strength advantage, the winner would almost certainly be determined by skill rather than sheer strength. If you put even the strongest of Neanderthals in a ring with a professional MMA fighter, the Neanderthal would be at a disadvantage because of the MMA fighter's extensive training and skill. On the other hand, if you gave the Neanderthal his (or her) weapon of choice, such as an ax (khul) or spear, the Neanderthal would have the advantage due to extensive experience and skill with the weapon. Skyra is a skilled hunter, and she has fought raiding bolup men, so she is a formidable opponent. Her twin sister Veenah, although also somewhat skilled, has never been as interested as Skyra in hunting and fighting, therefore her level of skill may be lower. I wouldn't mess with either of them.

Why do you use the word human only for Homo sapiens in this story?

My use of the word *human* is a matter of preference. To make it easier to describe the characters, I use the word *human* to refer only to *Homo sapiens*. Some people choose to use *human* to refer to any hominid species in the genus *Homo*. Humans and Neanderthals are closely related and are classified in the same genus (*Homo sapiens* and *Homo neanderthalensis*), but they are considered two distinct species.

Skyra, and the other people who live in the Dofusofu river plain during her time, refer to humans as *bolups* and Neanderthals as *nandups*.

Are any of the Neanderthal tribal customs depicted in the story real? For example, Osroc's tribe sends their elderly tribemates away to die in the wilderness. Also, in Skyra's tribe, when a woman has seen twenty cold seasons, the dominant men of the tribe "challenge each other to put a child in her belly."

Neanderthals are extinct, and we know little about their tribal customs. Therefore, I created customs that I thought were realistic as well as interesting. Although obviously not legal in any society today, the killing of the elderly, known as *Senicide*, is thought to have occurred in ancient times in a variety of cultures worldwide. As you can imagine, this likely happened more frequently during times of famine and in tribes that regularly migrated great distances by foot, making it especially difficult for the elderly. That's the specific scenario with Osroc's tribe—they regularly move their camp as they follow the reindeer.

The mating ritual of Skyra's tribe is a bit more of a stretch. I do not know of any human society in which the men physically challenge each other for the right to mate with females (although it could be argued that men compete in other, less violent, ways for the attention of women, such as personal grooming and appearance, flaunting their wealth, and more). However, Neanderthals are not human (*Homo sapiens*), and there are numerous examples of non-human mammals in which males physically challenge each other for mates. Deer and bighorn sheep are well-known examples. Anyway, I thought it would be interesting if Skyra's tribe practiced such a custom.

Jazzlyn, Derek, and Virgil are important characters in the other books, yet they are hardly mentioned in Lincoln's chapter of this book. Why?

Jazzlyn, Derek, and Virgil are Lincoln's employees in the other books. Keep in mind that Lincoln is fourteen years older in *Genesis Sequence* (and in a different timeline). In this timeline, during the last fourteen years, Lincoln has grown reclusive and has fired most of his employees who used to work in close proximity with him. He has fired Jazzlyn and Derek, but he still needs Virgil around, as Virgil is essential to the operation of the T3 equipment. As Maddy stated, this version of Lincoln has become rather grouchy.

Now that this book and the four main books of the series are complete, will you write more Across Horizons stories?

It's possible, although currently I am working on other books. What would motivate me to write more stories related to the Across Horizons series? Readers, because my readers always motivate me. If readers demand more, I may write more—specifically, several related short stories and/or novellas. I'd love to know your ideas about possible stories and characters to expand this series. Which aspects of this series would you want to read more about?

Here are a few questions submitted to me from early readers of this book:

From Tammy Fiess and Christina Elnicki: *Did you already have this prequel in mind when you wrote the other books, or is it something that came to you after you already started the series?*

I planned out this entire series before I started writing the first book **Obsolete Theorem**. That is not to say that I planned the five books in great detail. I planned less than one page of details for each of the books, just enough to know the overall story arc. For me, the best ideas come during the endless hours of writing, so I like to make the series and book outlines relatively brief. This allows me to incorporate new ideas as they come to me, and all five of these books ended up being quite different from what I initially envisioned, which is fine. I knew from the beginning that I wanted to write a prequel, and I knew the prequel would tell the story of how Skyra meets Ripple (although at the time I didn't know their names would be Skyra and Ripple). I did not yet know that the book's major conflict would be Skyra's struggle to find her strength.

After I completed **Binary Existence**, the final book of the main 4-book series, it was time to write the prequel. I already knew Skyra had met Ripple two years before Obsolete Theorem takes place, so I knew Skyra and Veenah would have to be eighteen years old. I also knew their birthmother Sayleeh had died about a year previously, when the girls were seventeen, and I knew Sayleeh's death had been really hard on the twins. I even knew Skyra would eventually find the woolly rhino that killed her birthmother. So, it seemed logical to create a storyline around all this. That's where Skyra's struggle to find her strength comes from. I love witty, well-written dialogue, so I decided this story needed more characters in addition to just Skyra and Ripple (although those two have a lot of fun conversations together). The solution? Bring in Osroc. Another solution? Have Ripple create at least one alternate personality within its cognitive module, with which it could converse. After all, this was my first opportunity to show what goes on inside Ripple's "mind," and I wanted to make it interesting and surprising. The result, I hope, is a lot of interesting and funny exchanges between five characters instead of only two.

Also, I thought it would be fun to build anticipation and suspense for an epic, climactic battle between Skyra and the pack of cave hyenas but then throw in a surprise twist, having the climactic battle take place with a band of ruthless bolups (humans) instead.

Now that all five novels are complete, I think that if I were to sit down and read all of them back-to-back, I would prefer to read books 1, 2, 3, and 4 first, then read the prequel **Genesis Sequence**.

From Jenny Avery: *Why did you choose that particular time period?*

This entire story is initiated when Dr. Mottram and Dr. Dunkley get a research grant to collect data in a specific location and time in which Neanderthals lived. They chose Spain as the location due to the abundance of Neanderthal remains that have been found in the targeted area. They choose 47,675 years in the past because that was a time when we know Neanderthals existed in Spain. The *exact* year is more-or-less arbitrary. Mottram and Dunkley knew there was only a slight chance that the drone (Ripple) would actually encounter a Neanderthal during the brief, 19-minute window in which the portal would be open. However, they would still learn a great deal about the environment Neanderthals existed in by having Ripple collect data from the immediate area around the portal.

Also from Jenny Avery: *What's the difference between saber-toothed tigers that we have all heard of and scimitar-toothed cats described in this book?*

You are right—the "saber-toothed tiger" is known by most people, whereas the scimitar-toothed cat is lesser known. However, the saber-toothed cat (Smilodon) lived in the Americas. The scimitar-toothed cat (Homotherium) lived in the Americas, too, but also in Eurasia and Africa. Since the story takes place in Spain, I used the scimitar-toothed cat, for the sake of accuracy.

Notice that above I replaced saber-toothed *tiger* with saber-toothed *cat*. This is because tiger is a somewhat misleading name because these creatures were not closely related to tigers at all.

Both of these cats were about the size of a modern lion, and the scimitar-toothed cat had canine teeth that, although they were really long, were not as long as the 11-inch (28 cm) canines of the saber-toothed cat. Regardless, they both had powerful jaws and were deadly predators.

From Lisa Ensign: *Skyra recognizes the voices of nandups and bolups, even if she doesn't know the words being spoken. Aren't humans and Neanderthals similar? Would they not have similar voices?*

We can learn about the sounds of voices by comparing the hyoid bones of humans and Neanderthals. The hyoid bone is a horseshoe-shaped bone in the throat that supports the root of the tongue, and its shape and placement is a large part of what allows us to speak. We can also reconstruct the shape of a Neanderthal's throat and vocal tract. These can be built virtually and with physical materials. The results of such studies indicate it is likely that Neanderthals had voices that were higher-pitched than human voices. Not only that, but their deep, powerful chests and large nasal cavities would give their voice a strange, very loud, nasally sound. In other words, they probably had voices we would immediately recognize as different from ours (and vice versa). This is why, when Skyra accidentally speaks words from within her "suit of armor," she realizes the bolup men could hear that she was a nandup rather than a bolup or some other creature.

Finally, here's a comment from Eugenia Kollia: *The end of the book, I think, needs a sequel. I would like to see how Ripple devised the plan to bring the heroes together, as well as how Ripple bonded its friendship with Skyra.*

Yes, this would be a fun story to write (and to read). Somehow, for almost two years, Skyra manages to keep Ripple a secret from her sister and her entire tribe. She is afraid her tribemates will destroy Ripple if they find out. She's probably right about that, but how does she keep Ripple secret for so long, especially when she goes to visit the drone on a regular basis? What other adventures do Skyra and Ripple have together during those two years? How does Ripple manage to teach Skyra to speak English? Do more bolup hunters ever come to the area to find their missing tribemates?

Also, what happened to Lincoln to make him the way he is? How did he create the amazing T3? How did he create Maddy and decide to make her his friend?

There are plenty of questions that would be fun to answer. However, there are so many other stories I want to write... other universes, other strange creatures, other dangers, and other relationships. I love hearing story ideas from readers, so let me know if you have some for the Across Horizons series.

ACKNOWLEDGMENTS

I am not capable of creating a book such as this on my own. I have the following people, among others, to thank for their assistance.

First I wish to thank Monique Agueros for her help with editing. She has a keen eye for typos, poorly structured sentences, misplaced commas, and errors of logic. If you find a sentence or detail in the book that doesn't seem right, it is likely because I failed to implement one of her suggestions.

My wife Trish is always the first to read my work, and therefore she has the burden of seeing my stories in their roughest form. Thankfully, she kindly points out where things are a mess. Her suggestions are what get the editing process started. She also helps with various promotional efforts. And finally, she not only tolerates my obsession with writing, she actually encourages it.

I also owe thanks to those on my Advance Reviewer team. They were able to point out numerous typos and inconsistencies, and they are all-around fabulous people!

Finally, I am thankful to all the independent freelance designers out there who provide quality work for independent authors such as myself. Jake Caleb Clark (www.jcalebdesign.com) created the awesome cover for *Genesis Sequence*.

ABOUT THE AUTHOR

Stan Smith has lived most of his life in the Midwest United States and currently resides with his wife Trish in a house deep in an Ozark forest in Missouri. He writes adventure novels that have a generous sprinkling of science fiction. His novels and stories are about regular people who find themselves caught up in highly unusual situations. They are designed to stimulate your sense of wonder, get your heart pounding, and keep you reading late into the night, with minimal risk of exposure to spelling and punctuation errors. His books are for anyone who loves adventure, discovery, and mind-bending surprises.

Stan's Author Website
http://www.stancsmith.com

Feel free to email Stan at: stan@stancsmith.com
He loves hearing from readers and will answer every email.

ALSO BY STAN C. SMITH

The DIFFUSION series

Diffusion

Infusion

Profusion

Savage

Blue Arrow

Diffusion Box Set

The BRIDGERS series

Bridgers 1: The Lure of Infinity

Bridgers 2: The Cost of Survival

Bridgers 3: The Voice of Reason

Bridgers 4: The Mind of Many

Bridgers 5: The Trial of Extinction

Bridgers 6: The Bond of Absolution

INFINITY: A Bridger's Origin

Bridgers 1-3 Box Set

Bridgers 4-6 Box Set

The ACROSS HORIZONS series

1: Obsolete Theorem

2. Foregone Conflict

3. Hostile Emergence

4. Binary Existence

Prequel: Genesis Sequence

The FUSED series

Prequel: Training Day

1. Rampage Ridge

2. Primordial Pit

Stand-alone Stories

Parthenium's Year

Printed in Great Britain
by Amazon